Cover design by: Rebecca Matthew
Library of Congress Control Number: 2018675309
Printed in the United States of America

The Rapture of the Deep is dedicated to my children—they are the reason I write, they are the reason I live.

There is no greatness where simplicity, goodness, and truth do not exist.

LEO TOLSTOY

CONTENTS

1. HIS NAME IS NUKILIK

Elissa doubles over and moans, a small sickening

sound, low and guttural, like an animal. She cannot get comfortable in such a confined space, with barely a hands-width between her and the man in the window seat beside her. In this moment, she feels more animal than human and maybe in this most primal act of birth, it is the animal that takes over. Maybe there is no difference, now, between her and the bear or the moose or the calving whale.

But these are thoughts for later. Now, she is consumed by the pain. The man seated next to her, so close she can see the small beads of sweat glistening on his forehead, looks at her warily, as if he thinks she will bite him, and maybe she will. Her sister bit her brother-in-law while she was contracting with their first baby. Bit him hard enough to break skin. To taste blood. Elissa almost laughs, picturing herself looking at the man and baring her teeth. Then another roll of contractions comes, and she thinks only of the pain.

The baby is too early. Too early by three months. The insurance company booked her a flight to Anchorage for the end of May, a month before she was due, but it was not early enough. Now, she will not be able to graduate. She will never graduate. She will end up, the same as her mother, as both of her sisters, as her grandmother before them, stuck in a village too small to be even a speck on a map, repeating a never-ending cycle of life, birth, and death. She feels the baby twist inside of her and the edge of an elbow or heel pushing taut against her. She rubs at the spot until the pressure subsides. She smiles. “Not much longer little Katsi,” she whispers. It is the first time she says the name aloud, and it feels good, it feels right.

The man (who said his name was David) glances over, as if he thinks she is talking to him. “Excuse me? Are you okay?" He has on a collared shirt, black slacks, black boots that aren't scuffed. He is not from around here. No one dresses like that, not even the principal at her school. Elissa's eyes open wider, the whites bulging around the oval of green. She thinks she might pass out, and groans again, clutching the man's arm, digging her fingers into his soft flesh. He looks down at her hand and then at her face, distorted by pain. She sees horror in his face and thinks it is because he's afraid of her. Like most men, afraid of this whole process.

But she is mistaken. It isn't horror or fear, it is compassion. He tells her, in a low, soothing voice, that he has a daughter about her age. A girl going to Harvard in the fall. "I don't think you should be flying in your state," he says. Elissa can see in his eyes, which look quickly away from her, that he knows it is precisely the wrong thing to say. She glares at him, then notices, for the first time, that she is gripping his arm, and pulls her hand away. "I'm sorry," she says. "There's no doctor to deliver a preemie in my village, or a hospital to take care of her after the birth. We're usually flown to Anchorage the month before we're expected to deliver. I didn't think the baby would come so early." She doesn't know if the apology is for his arm or for the baby that might come while they are in transit.

"I'll get you some water," he says, wanting to be useful, and presses the call button above his head.

***

Nine months earlier, a baby was the farthest thing from Elissa's mind. Nine months earlier she met Roland. Elissa is a senior. Her mother made it to fourth grade. Her oldest sister to ninth. The middle sister to tenth.

She will be the first of the family's girls to have a high-school diploma. And with a high school diploma, college might be a possibility. The barest, slimmest one, but still a possibility.

It is a gray, heavy day. The clouds seem to press against the windows of the classroom. Elissa can picture them sliding under the gap at the base of the door and filling the room with fog. The teacher's hair is damp with it, and he pushes thick bangs from his eyes. She knows he watches her and finds she is pleased. She is a slender girl, straight black hair to her waist, flawless olive complexion, wide nose and oval face. In these things she is nearly identical to every other girl that has walked into his class that morning. It is her eyes, she knows, that catch him off guard. They are a pale green, like the flesh of a manzanilla olive. He watches her as she slings her worn yellow bookbag over the back of her seat. She sits in the middle of the room. Precisely in the middle. She wears a heavy wool sweater, cream flecked with gray. When a couple of the boys look at her, and one, who was sitting in the back, moves to a desk near hers, she watches from the corner of her eye to see if the teacher notices. She pretends to be unaware of their attention. She settles herself into the seat, arranging a notebook and pencil on her desk, pulling her long hair over one shoulder. Then, she looks up, and their eyes meet. It is Roland who looks away, embarrassed that she saw him watching her.

Elissa notices everything. Nukilik, or Nuk Nuk, which is what they have all called him since kindergarten, moves his things to a seat behind hers. She feels his eyes on her back. He smells like smoke and animal fur. He's big for his age, and he's let his hair grow over the summer, so it hangs to his earlobes. It is thick and black, like hers. His eyebrows are thick and black too, and he has full lips and a strong jaw. Last year, he wrote her a poem. It was sweet, but terrible. Something about hunting caribou. It was supposed to mirror his feelings for her in some obscure way. He could probably have any girl in the class. Any girl (or woman) in the village. He just needs to be more confident. He is a sure-fire way to never leave this place. She can see his life stretched before her in every village alcoholic father with their five ambling offspring. She knows that, last year, he came to class stoned at least twice a week. Those were the only days he worked up the courage to talk to her.

And, of course, she also notices the teacher. When he looks away, she does not.

When it appears most of the seats are full, and he has taken roll, Roland turns and writes his name on the blackboard. Elissa notices, with a small smile to herself, that he almost forgets and writes Mr. Finnigan. She notices because all of the new teachers do this. As with so many of their village customs, students using the teacher's first name is foreign to them. He remembers at the M, erasing it to write Roland, Physics I. Later, when Elissa tries to figure everything out, she thinks this is part of the problem. It is too much familiarity for him. Too little distance between teacher and student. Nothing formal to find your bearings with. The small act of using the first name throws everything off. It makes them equals.

It is not difficult to learn about someone in a village of four hundred. The most interesting thing that happens every year is the arrival of the new teachers. Young and idealistic, they are gone by the following fall, many by

Christmas break. Only the two thousand dollar bonus convinces them to stick it out for the full year. She learns, from Kireama, that he moved here from New York. Not the city New York, but a place where there are apple trees and cows that is still called New York. Her sister, Meriwa, tells her that he left behind a fiancé. Who dumped who, she has not learned yet. Pilip, her brother-in-law, tells them all that he comes from money, that his father is an actor. Elissa, slowly, pieces together a picture of him. Someone with an adventurous spirit, an intellectual who wants a life bigger, fuller than his father's. A dreamer whose heart was broken by a beautiful, vapid girl. A girl that did not appreciate him.

***

Nukilik hates when they call him Nuk Nuk. Nukilik means one who is strong, Nuk Nuk is a dumb sound made with the mouth. It means nothing. If he were someone else, he would tell them to stop with a single firm word and a shake of his fist, but that is not him. Despite his intimidating size, he knows no one is afraid of him. Once, and only once, when she called him Nuk Nuk, he said very quietly, "It's Nukilik."

She laughed at him. "You can't change your name now, silly." Then, seeing his face darken, she added, "The name suits you, it's sweet."

As usual, Nukilik didn't know whether she was complimenting or insulting him. He just knew he wanted her to think of him as a man, not a sweet boy. He never tried to correct her again, though.

He knows that he's not the only one mooning over Elissa. There's always been something different about her, something unlike any of the other village girls. She holds herself a little apart, whether intentionally or not, she is distinctive. "A rare bird," his cousin said once, eyeing her in a way that made Nukilik's heart race, made him watch her protectively whenever his cousin was near. She was smart, ambitious, and she had those eyes. They said her great-grandfather had the same eyes, and he was the last one from their village to leave and never come back.

Nukilik likes to think he loves her for reasons better than theirs. He loves how she notices everything and everyone. How she knows, without being told, when his father has been in a rage, and gently pats his arm as she walks by. How she loops her long hair around her thumb and index finger when she's daydreaming. How her favorite nephew is the one with the birth-mark covering half of his face, and she is his favorite aunt. No one else will ever know her so well, he thinks, and perhaps he is right.

Nukilik sees how she never takes her eyes from that teacher the first day. Then, over the next few weeks, he sees other things. The teacher, stepping close to her desk, brushes the tips of her fingers with his. Tucks a flower in the corner of her desk. Puts his hand on the small of her back, absently, as if touching her this way were nothing. One day, Nukilik comes back to get a book from the classroom, and Elissa is leaning over Roland's desk. Her cheeks flare pink when she sees him, and she hurries out, glancing back once at the door. Her eyes, shining and alive, are not for Nukilik. He watches all of these things, his heart constricting. He doesn't know what he is supposed to do.

***

It is two weeks before Roland invites her to his

home. She knows he wants to come sooner, but needs to find a plausible reason. She feigns confusion on the topic of vectors, though they both know it to be a ruse. He tells her to come by his home where they can work through a few of the problems together.

She knows where he lives. It is the plain, two-story, narrow-windowed row of teacher apartments across the street from the school. Beneath her sweater she wears a black lace camisole, belonging to her sister Meriwa. Meriwa will notice it is gone, but Elissa does not care.

Roland is sitting on the couch when she enters, bent over a stack of papers. He puts down the red marking pen and stands to greet her. His eyes scan her and she sees the blush beneath his collar. This pleases her, knowing she makes him nervous. Knowing she has this power.

She sits close enough to him that their legs touch at the seam. The room is small and dim. He has closed the blinds, which are made to black out the never-ending sun of mid-winter. One small lamp is turned on in the corner. Its light is soft and makes shadows against the pale wall.

They play at working through two problems before he kisses her. It is a hesitant kiss, a soft kiss, at first. She leans into him, pressing herself closer, making him know this is what she wants. It is enough. They have both wanted this since that first day.

By late fall, when the first snow comes and the sea begins to freeze, she knows he is too far in to see what has happened. For her part, Elissa knows she has bewitched him. Sometimes he whispers to her that when she graduates, he might be able to take her back with him to Syracuse. His mother will love her. His father and friends will be scandalized.

"You barely look a day over fifteen," he says, kissing her, trying to smile, trying to laugh about it.

Jamie, the once-fiancé, will be furious. Jamie is the reason, Elissa understands deep down, that bringing her back will be impossible.

It is in November that Elissa tells him about the baby. She lies on her back with her head resting on his stomach, her slim ankles crossed by the foot of the bed. He circles one finger around the outline of her brown nipple. She turns, so she can look at him, her chin on his chest, hair spilling like a blanket around her shoulders.

"I'm pregnant," she says. Just like that, with nothing building up to it, nothing to warn him. One moment peace, the next an explosion. He looks at her for a moment, then quickly away. She sees it in that fleeting look, the feeling of sickening déja vu. Jamie had said the same to him. Roland told this to Elissa, one night when she lay beside him. Told her of the baby they were not ready for. Jamie had more finesse. She knew how to break it to him gently. Elissa knows she is too direct.

"We can't have a baby," he says, as gently as possible, and tries to kiss her. She sits up before his lips reach her mouth. Another woman might have thrown on clothes, or left, angry. She only looks at him. She sits perfectly still and looks. As on the first day they met, he is the one to look away. This time it is shame.

"There must be someone here who can take care of it?"

"There isn't," she says.

"Well, Anchorage then, I'll pay for the flight. I'm sure

we can come up with a reasonable explanation."

"No."

"What?" He pauses. "Surely you can't mean? You can't...We can't..." his voice trails off as he looks at her. She is sitting straight up now, her legs crossed and her hands resting on her bare knees. Her eyes are wide and clear.

"I will have the baby," she says.

He begins to plead, to grovel, to manipulate. She will ruin him, he says. He'll be fired. He'll go to jail. His family will never speak to him again. He goes on and on. She notices he does not once mention what will happen to her.

"Okay," he says, finally, when he has exhausted himself and she still has not spoken, "what about Nuk Nuk?"

She looks at him, confused, but only for a moment. Her eyes become slits. "I will not do that."

He watches her dress, jeans first, then bra clipped in the back, then sweater pulled over the head. Her hair looks short, tucked in beneath the opening of the sweater. It makes her seem older. She opens the door to the porch where her coat hangs and as she leaves he calls after her.

"Just think about it? Please? For me?" He is not sure if she hears him. The wind slams the door shut with a loud bang, and she is gone.

Two days later, there is a knock on the door, and when Nukilik answers it he is surprised to find Elissa there. She wears only a thin turtleneck over black leggings, and is shivering. He brings her inside, through the living room, where his parents and siblings are watching Family

Feud, to the back bedroom that he shares with two younger brothers. They sit on opposite ends, at the foot of his bed. She looks at her hands, and he looks at her.

“Are you okay?” he says, finally.

She does not answer, but looks up at him and begins to cry. His arms are too big, he thinks, as he tries to wrap them around her, his hands too clumsy, as he tries to stroke her hair.

Then, she is kissing him. On the mouth, then the throat, then beneath his shirt, then in the places he hardly dared to imagine she would ever be. When they are done, she dresses silently, and leaves without looking at him. He realizes, then, that she came and went without saying a single word.

***

In February, it is only just getting light out at noon. As they land, the sun can be seen, a dull haze of orange on the horizon, half a sphere fighting through thick, white cloud. It is snowing. Large, soft flakes that soon shrink in size and increase in number. There is an ambulance waiting. The man named David offers to carry her off the plane. She does not refuse him. At the door, she passes out, her head lulling to one side on his shoulder. No one questions him when he gets into the ambulance with her, his bag forgotten on the tarmac.

At the hospital, David finds himself saying he is her father, and someone ushers him to a seat in the hallway outside her room. Someone else brings him coffee. Black and strong, a layer of slush at the bottom. He listens to her moaning, then screaming. He watches doctors and nurses rush in and out. Finally, there is quiet. He waits for the sounds of a baby crying.

***

"You can hold her, if you want," says the nurse. "Sometimes it helps."

Elissa nods, and the nurse places the child in her arms. She is no larger than one of Elissa's palms. Her skin is translucent, thin, and soft, like the petals of an orchid. Elissa kisses her head, and her eyes, which the nurse has closed. She pulls down the gown, as she has seen her mother and sisters do, and presses the tiny mouth to her breast.

"Now, now," says the nurse, clucking softly, "that's not going to help. It's best just to say goodbye. Here, I'll take her." She reaches out both hands with a tired, tender expression.

Elissa pulls back, clutching the baby against her.

"No," she says, looking fiercely at the woman.

The nurse sighs. "I'll be right back." She steps into the hallway and finds the man still sitting there.

"How is she?" he asks, standing.

"She's fine," says the nurse, pausing for only a moment. "But your granddaughter didn't make it—I'm so sorry."

He looks at her, unravelling what she has said. "Can I see her?"

"Yes," says the woman. "Yes, of course."

The room is very small, but bright. All the frenzy and blood of the birth have been cleaned away. It smells sterile, lifeless. The man looks at the girl, covered to the chin with a blue sheet. He can see the tiny thing clutched to her chest, beneath the cover. Her hair is damp and her eyes look wild and dark, like a deer or a small birds'.

"I'll leave you two alone," says the nurse, closing the door with a soft click behind her. Four steps take him to Elissa's side. She looks up at him and smiles.

"Do you want to hold her?" she says, cheerfully.

"Okay."

She pulls back the cover and places the child in his hands. They form a perfect cradle around her body. He feels something slick and salty slide into the corner of his mouth, and realizes he is crying.

"She's so beautiful, isn't she?" the girl whispers.

"Yes," he says. "Does she have a name?"

"Katsi. It means precious flower."

"That's perfect," he tells her. "The perfect name."

They stand like this, for a minute, then she reaches out her hands, and he places the baby back into her arms.

"Is there anyone you want me to call?" he says, quietly. "Anyone who might come?"

The girl stares at him, and he notices that her eyes have cleared. They are bright and focused, seeming to reflect the room's light. She thinks for a moment. Two faces held tight in her mind. The pale, smooth-cheeked face of Roland, and the sun-browned somber-faced Nukilik. She can hear Roland's voice, when she called him on her way to the airport.

"You know I can't, Elissa. You have to understand. There would be too many questions if I went with you." He paused, and for a moment she thought, or hoped, he was still considering. "I'm sorry," he said, and then there was silence. He was gone.

"Yes," Elissa says, in answer to David, "you can call Nuk Nuk." Then she pauses, considering. "No," she says, "Not Nuk Nuk—Nukilik. His name is Nukilik. This is his daughter."

***

Elissa is not able to let the baby go. The nurse would have had to pry the child from her arms, and chooses not to do this, believing Elissa will let go on her own, in her own time. The baby is swaddled tightly in a pink hospital blanket, so to an unquestioning eye she appears every bit the living creature Elissa so longs for her to be. On the airplane, no one questions her, and a few people even smile, offering their congratulations.

In the village, Elissa sees the villagers, her classmates, her teachers, her friends. They cross the street when they notice her. They whisper together, huddled in a tight crescent, their faces bent away from her. She does not return to school.

Nukilik comes every day. He knocks. "I'm here to see Elissa," he tells her mother when she opens the door. His voice is husky, awkward. Mother looks at him. There is sorrow and understanding in her eyes.

"I'm sorry," she says, "she's not ready yet."

He sits on the steps, often in the snow. He waits. An hour. Sometimes two. Then he walks home, his head bent, his feet shuffling.

But one day, she lets him in. It is more than a week. Mother takes him to her room. He has not seen it before. He has never even been in the house, only glimpsed it through the open front door. It is a clean room. The bed is made. White sheets and a white comforter. Elissa sits at a desk. It is dark wood. Her back is to him. Her hair is loose, cascading down her back. Black as licorice. Her foot is against the side of the bassinet. She rocks it with delicate, precise movements. She is humming. The window is open and there is a mound of fresh snow at its lip. Nukilik steps toward her. His heart thuds dully in his chest. She turns and smiles at him.

Her lips are blue but her cheeks are flushed. She is dressed for the outdoors, and Nukilik realizes she must never close the window. He knows why, but tries not to think it. He sits on the bed, near her.

"I'm glad you're here," she says. She stops rocking the baby, and moves beside him. She takes his hand. They sit like this for a long time.

"Can I see her?" he says, finally.

"Of course," she smiles, squeezing his hand, then releasing it. They go together, to stand by the child.

She is covered completely with the blanket, nothing more than the outline of a baby. But he can picture her, and she is perfect. Her eyes are closed, he thinks, and he can imagine them. They are the same as her mother's. Green as glass. She is so small beneath her pink cover. Smaller than he would even have thought possible. Her tiny hands are hidden beneath her blanket, but he can picture them too. Fists balled, ready for the world. Elissa rests her head on his shoulder. He thinks she is crying. He knows that he is.

"I want to have a funeral," she says. "And then, I want to marry you."

She turns her head to him. There are no tears, her eyes are liquid. He bends down, kissing her once on her upturned mouth.

***

The village comes to the wedding. It is a thing not to be missed. Roland is there. Not to come would be to bring gossip. He finds her before the ceremony. She is dressed simply. A gown of smooth ivory. A single string of pearls at her throat. Her hair pinned at the nape of her neck with a silver barrette.

"I've missed you," he says. "Are you sure this is what you want?" And then in a rush, as if his mouth is speaking before his mind can catch up, "You can come back with me. I'd marry you. We could have another baby."

When she turns, it is obvious that he is shocked by the change. She is no longer a girl. She opens her mouth to answer, then closes it again. She has nothing to say to him. He starts to nod, his head lifting, stopping halfway on the downward motion.

There is someone else in the room. Someone in the corner whose form emerges from the shadow. It is Nukilik.

Roland's breath catches. He tries to swallow but there is not enough saliva. Nukilik takes a step toward him. Then another. Roland backs toward the open door. Nukilik can see the sweat forming on his brow, pooling in dark patches beneath his arms. He might turn and run. He might scream. Nukilik hopes for this. Then, he will chase him down, hunt him like the caribou. This is a situation he understands. It is the way of this place. It is his right.

But the man is rendered mute. He is rendered immobile. Nukilik towers over him.

"You don't belong here," he says, his voice soft but clear as a flute. "Go home."

Roland turns, his legs coming to life again, but still he doesn't move. He glances at Elissa. She does not look at him.

"GO!" Nukilik commands, now a bugle.

Roland runs.

***

When David calls her, it is nearly fall again. She knows his voice at once. They have spoken regularly over the past year. He has become father and friend. "How are you?" he asks. It is true concern.

"I'm good," she tells him. "I'm married."

"That's wonderful," he says. "He'd better treat you well."

"He does," she says, simply, and he can hear the smile in her voice.

"What are you going to do?" he asks. For a moment, she is confused by the question.

"I don't know," she says, understanding. "I don't think I can just go back. I don't belong in a high school anymore."

"That's what I thought." He pauses, considering his words. "That's why I'm calling. I've talked to my wife. We want you to come here. To Boston," he reminds her, incase she's forgotten. "You could go to school and live with us. You and your husband, of course. We have the room. We've talked to our daughter too, she likes the idea. You'd be like sisters."

Elissa is silent. Silent long enough that he thinks he may have lost her. But then, she speaks.

"I think," she says, a whisper of a sound, "I think I would like that. I would like that very much."

But then she thinks of Nukilik. She tries to picture him, towering like a gnarled tree over the manicured city. No sea to fish. No caribou to hunt. Dressed in slacks and tidy, uncuffed shoes. He will be lost. She will lose him. She takes a breath. One breath. That's all she needs.

"I can't," she says. "I'm sorry."

"Perhaps… in another life," he says, trying to make his voice light.

"Yes," she agrees. "Perhaps."

***

In the night, he comes to her. When he lies next to her, a warm, solid weight at her side, she does not tell him about the phone call. Instead, she pulls his hands across her, places them on her stomach, just below the dimple of her belly button. She makes her body form to the contours of his, and she tells him about the baby. When she told him, before the wedding, after Roland left, that Katsi was not his, he had pulled her close, saying only, "You are wrong."

This time, it will be their baby in truth. "If it's a boy," she says, kissing his rough cheek, "I want to name him Nukilik." When Nukilik laughs, it is the sound of rain through the whispering trees. It is the waterfall on the mountain. It is the sea ice cracking beneath the strain of the sun. Elissa places her head on his chest, feeling the laugh course through him.

"It's a good name," she says, though he has not spoken. "It is the name of the man I love."

They lie in silence, hardly daring to breathe. Hardly daring to move. Beyond their window, the wind whistles its cold song across the barren, frozen earth. The sound is soothing. It is the sound of this place. The sound of their home. Joy fills Nukilik, spilling out, radiating through his fingers and scalp. Making his whole body alive. Alive in a way he has never felt before. He knows there is nothing else he needs. He kisses the top of her head, once. When she looks at him, her eyes shine. Momentarily, he wonders if they are tears. He remembers her grandfather. The last person who left the village. A tiny sliver of pain shoots through the joy. He will not be enough for her, he thinks. This place will not be enough. He does not have the words to tell her what he knows, and so he is silent.

In the morning she wakes and he is gone. The Honda is gone, and his fishing gear. The ice is still too thin. It is too early in the season. She is afraid. She frets at home all day, not wanting to make a fuss and embarrass him. When evening begins to throw its gloved hand over the landscape outside her window, she can wait no longer and calls.

"He left early this morning before I got up," she tells his father, who is calm, even though he knows. He knows what happens on this ice. It cannot hold against five hundred pounds of snowmobile and man.

Meriwa comes to sit with Elissa. She is a good sister. She holds her hand. She distracts her with gossip. “Did you know that teacher, Roland, left?” she asks, looking at Elissa from the corner of her dark eye.

Elissa stares at her hands and Meriwa continues. “He had a contract for the new year but never showed up at the school. When they finally got in touch with him, he told them he got married and wasn’t coming back. Crazy, huh?”

“Why would he do this?” Elissa asks, eyes turned to the window again.

“Oh, you know, white folks are weak, none of them can handle it here. Same old story.”

“What? What are you talking about?” Elissa looks at her sister, startled. “I’m talking about Nukilik,” she says. “He knows better than to go out on the ice when it’s still so warm. Why would he do it? I just can’t understand.”

Meriwa reaches out and rubs the back of her sister’s neck. The muscles are hard with tension.

“I don’t know. I’ve never been able to figure men out.”

***

It is midnight when the light from a truck appears in the dark, glowing on the snow, in the black. It stops before the house. Meriwa is asleep on the bed and wakes when she hears the front door slam. She can see Elissa standing, barefoot, in the snow. She is opening the back door of the truck, climbing in. Nukilik’s father steps down from the front seat and she watches him walk to the front door, glancing back once. The truck is still running, the lights making two circles of white against the house.

Nukilik is in the back. He is sleeping. His face is flushed to rust red. The heat in the car is turned to furnace strength. Elissa pulls his head into her lap, wiping the damp hair away from his face. He feels her there, but does not move. Her long hair tickles his cheek and he can smell her, fresh as summer wind. "Don't you ever do something like that again," she says, her wet face pressed against his forehead. "Do you hear me? Don't you ever do that again."

That night, Elissa dreams. It is many years later. She has just retired from her position as the beloved high school English teacher. Nukilik's hair is gray and he walks with a limp from an old hunting injury. Their daughter lives in Philadelphia, but comes home for most holidays. Their son lives with his wife and children in Anchorage. If it is cold enough, the sea a frozen wasteland, they can drive across to visit him.

Today, though, they make a picnic. Chunks of preserved salmon, a heel of hard bread, the final jar of jam from last season, two cans of beer. The sky is a dome of blue, spreading forever, merging into the sea and the deeper blue of the mountain. The sun is fighting its way through the morning chill. It seems it may win today. It is warm enough, as they climb the mountain, that they both remove their heavy coats, tying them snugly around their waists. They move slowly, not speaking.

In a few hours, when they reach the top, Elissa sits and closes her eyes. She can feel Nukilik breathing beside her. Deep, rumbling, bear breaths. She takes his hand, her eyes still closed. Joy, pure, clear, cold and calm as the surface of a lake. It saturates every fiber; she can feel it flowing from her, pulsing through her veins. Her blood is thick with it.

After lunch, they lie back in the fibrous grass and fall asleep. When they wake there is a wolf. They see it at nearly the same time. Together, they watch as its gray body, tense and muscled, lopes away beneath them, winding through the brush until it disappears from sight. Nukilik helps her up. Her back is stiff and there are bits of dry grass in her hair. They pack the remnants of their meal and head back, trailing a path parallel with the wolf's. In the distance, the village is visible, a series of stones against the flat tundra. Somewhere among those stones is their own. From here, its weathered, storm-peeled and warped walls sit smooth and white, glinting in the warmth of the afternoon sun.

When she wakes, she turns to find Nukilik beside her, and pushes the soft black hair gently away from his face, kissing him on the crease between his eyes. She wants to wake him, to make love to him. To tell him of the dream. She marvels at her contentment, that she does not, in this moment, long for anything more than what she saw in the dream. She nestles herself deeper into the warmth of his arm. It is enough.

2. TREKKING EVEREST

Hold fast to dreams, for if dreams die, life is a broken winged bird that cannot fly.

~Langston Hughes

Margot fully intended to go by herself. She already had her ticket, purchased two months ago, round trip to Kathmandu in June. She couldn't leave any sooner, since she didn't finish teaching until May 30th. It was also the latest she could go without being in danger of hitting monsoon season head-on. She'd been emailing with the tour company for several months and had a printed list of all the things she needed, which hung lopsided from the refrigerator door. Every time she thought of going to Starbucks for a cappuccino, she placed $5 in a trip-jar instead. She had a copy of Walt Unsworth's monumental *Everest*, hard-back and bound in blue, which she'd made it nearly half-way through. She'd read Jon Krakauer's *Into Thin Air* twice and rather than being deterred by the harrowing account, she'd become increasingly enamored by the prospect of her own adventure.

Her parents came, as they usually did, to stay with her and Tom and the kids for the Christmas break.

They already knew about her plans for the summer and had promised to come watch the children for the month she would be gone. Her father, a lean man of fifty-nine, was the third person she thought of asking to go. At fifty-nine, he could still do all the things a man of sixty could not. She asked her brothers first, but one could not get off work, or leave the girlfriend. The other had a wife, due with their baby in June. Her father was a teacher too, with the summers free, and, other than a few low points during adolescence, they had always gotten along well.

The bright spots in her childhood that she liked to daydream about were often moments with her dad. A walk along train tracks, balancing like a tightrope walker on the rails, catching hold of his hand for balance. A hike past a quarry filled with multi-colored layers of playdough-like clay that glistened in the Carolina sun. While her mother ran ahead, taking every trail like a marathon run, and the boys wrestled with each other, behind, she and her father meandered, discovering lichen, bird-print and skunk scat. He talked in a low and hushed voice, knowing the name of every species of plant, showing her how to spot the fuzzy vine of poison ivy, which mushrooms were edible and which would spout spores in a grey-green cloud, the milky white under-layer of bark on a Sycamore. Then, when he grew tired of talking, they walked in silence, and that was good too. So she knew hiking with him would be better than hiking alone. And in a way, perhaps, she felt it would be like taking a trip into the past, revisiting her childhood.

When she asked him, he said yes, without hesitation. For a moment her mother complained about being stuck watching the children without him, but quickly decided she'd prefer James to go with Margot than for Margot to go alone.

***

A red Hyundai hatchback waited for them at the airport. A smell of onions and diesel and sweat layered on top of sweet, steaming yak shit. The driver, who was also their guide, was not what either of them would have imagined. Of medium height, slightly overweight with a distinct paunch, it was difficult to picture him leading them for two weeks into the wilds of the Sagarmatha National Park.

That night, in the white hotel sheets, with the sounds of monkey chatter filtering through the open window, Margot dreamed of the children, of the baby, who was a toddler now, of her soft chubby arms, wrapped tightly around Margot's neck, and her sweet little mouth kissing her cheek. When she woke in the bright, cool morning, she had forgotten the dream, but had a furious longing to call home. Only the oldest was there when she called; the others had gone to the park with her mother. He sounded far away, through the phone, and it was difficult to picture him. What she'd really wished for was to hear the baby's happy chatter. They hung up and she washed her face and brushed her teeth.

On their tour of the city they passed two flour-skinned shamans, lounging in the dust by the road, clad in loincloths, eyes half closed, or rolled eerily back in their heads. Milan, their guide, told them, with a wicked, mischievous smile, that these men had reached the peak of holiness and no longer needed to be concerned with sin. They could eat flesh from the dead, practice Kamasutra with young virgins, dabble in hallucinogenics. Nothing was off limits for them. He laughed uproariously as they eyed the holy men warily and made a wide circle around them to cross the street. Twice that day they were almost hit by a car swerving rapidly in and out of the traffic that seemed to careen in ten different directions on the packed dirt roads. Once Margot was nearly bitten by a monkey, trying to snatch a bag of potato crisps from her hand.

After only two days, the city began to make her feel anxious and claustrophobic. The heat, the dust, the people, closing in on her like a thick wool blanket. And so it was with great relief that they stepped off the small cargo-plane with its flip-down seats and twelve passengers and into a cold, clear morning in Lukla. A small village spread below them; clusters of bright- roofed block-houses nestled between two ridges of mountains that sat in a narrow sweep of cloud. It was quiet and the air smelled fresh, sweet, cold. Margot breathed deeply and saw her dad was doing the same. They looked at each other and smiled. This was what they had been waiting for.

They shook hands with their porter over cups of watery, lukewarm Lipton tea. He was a slim, wide-eyed, beautiful boy of seventeen. They looked at him doubtfully. He would carry their packs ahead of them, waiting at the next tea-house while they labored in the thin mountain air. Milan assured them the boy was up to the task, mountain born, mountain bred, under the shadow of the Mother Mountain, under the shadow of Everest. And they watched with amazement over the next two-weeks as he leapt, agile as a mountain-goat, often reaching their next destination in half the time it took them.

The third day, they met two Dutch boys. The boys were friends, one tall, tan and blonde, the other short, muscular and dark. They were not much younger than Margot herself, but neither was married. The thought of children was so far from them that at first she felt that they had nothing in common with her. She spent mornings and evenings reading paperbacks filched from the leftovers of other trekkers. But she missed conversation and the boys, tired of one another, finally approached her. The blonde one, named Aert, offered to teach her to play Nerts (or Dutch Blitz) and Bram, the dark-haired, olive skinned one, joined in. They spent hours over the next week, each time they would meet at the next tea-house, playing and laughing and telling stories. At first, Margot felt awkward around them. She had never really spent much time in the company of men, other than her brothers, father, and husband. But gradually, their ease and good-humor won her over. They asked her questions about the children and told her stories of their adventures backpacking across Europe. Aert's eyes, she noticed, were the same color as the blue mountain sky they woke to each morning.

Her father, for his part, also made friends. In particular, a man, of an age with him, named Jesse. A wiry, divorced vagabond from North Carolina with a thick drawl and a bum knee. The two men often walked behind Margot and Milan, the soft drone of their conversation drifting like bird-song on the mountain air. Margot enjoyed the quiet, slow pace they kept. Often, Aert and Bram arrived with the porters, hours before them, already showered and hunched over their bowls of steaming Ramen. Margot and James's diet consisted nearly exclusively of thin tea, bowls of salty popcorn, and Ramen, and this was why, when others gorged on milky coffee and beef dumplings and became deathly ill, they were able to look on in sympathetic but unaffected silence.

It was not until the fifth day that they had their first glimpse of Everest. As the clouds slowly spread apart, a black needle of jagged rock emerged, tendrils of white snaking down its side, the sun a blinding circle behind it. Margot's breath caught and when she looked at her dad, she could see tears in his eyes, reflecting her own. They took a picture, the three of them standing in a row. Margot between James and Milan, arms draped around each other like old friends. Margot's dark hair was tucked under a wide-brim hat and only she smiled. The men wore serious, intent expressions, squinting against the glare of the sun which cast a sudden single, long beam of light directly in front of them, slicing between Margot and James and disappearing into the cobblestones.

The higher they climbed, the more the terrain changed with each day. The transformation was often drastic. Lush, green, verdant forest gave way to smaller and smaller growth, and dwarf-sized trees clinging unsteadily to rocky ledges became only rock, until finally, they were in a place that seemed to have more in common with the surface of the moon than the earth. Nothing living. Only boulder and rock and rushing, knife-cold, milky-blue water. They crossed bridges flung across wide gullies, swaying like a pendulum in the mountain wind, steadily focusing on the path in front, never the death-drop below. They wound for a full day on a dusty ledge with no shade and their lips began to crack and bleed and their nostrils filled with clay and airborne yak dung. They wrapped handkerchiefs around their noses and mouths, but still the dust won.

When they arrived at the last stop before their ascent to base camp, they found that Aert and Bram were suffering from mountain sickness, having pushed their bodies too hard. They both sat flushed, feverish and listless in the dark teahouse, unable to eat, hardly able to talk. Margot received a message from her husband saying that he missed her, that he could not find his keys that morning and had to hitchhike to work, that their daughter was bitten by a dog and the baby was getting two new teeth and did nothing but cry. Margot was unable to feel anything for him or the children. They seemed too far away, no longer her concern. Instead, she spent the evening nursing the Dutch boys. She spoonfed Aert Ramen broth, wiping Bram's forehead with a cool, damp cloth, and gave them both pills for altitude sickness from her own supply. At one point in the evening, Aert fell asleep with his blond head on her shoulder and she sat for a long time, not daring to move until her dad finally came, helping her lower him onto the bench and cover him with a wool blanket. In the morning, both boys were feeling better and sang the praises of Margot's nursing and swore to keep pace with her and James for the rest of the ascent.

They were up well before dawn the next day in order to climb a peak close by and watch the sun rise over Everest. At 18,000 feet, It was the highest they had climbed so far. Each step pushed Margot to the limits of what she thought she could bear. She had always believed that hiking was only a matter of one step following the next until the destination was reached. She only understood now how true that was. She shat herself, feeling each breath an ache, and then a screeching, blinding pain, and an effort not to vomit her organs. everything in her body was dissolving. But when she reached the top, she forgot everything. It was not Everest, but it might as well have been. She seemed to be perched on the very tip of the world, and Everest, still distant, seemed beneath her and not above, Hillary's pass visible as a smudge of snow no larger than the palm of her hand. They sat, each upon their own rock, balanced so precariously she felt the smallest breeze might topple any one of them over the edge.

Back at the tea house, she found it was her turn to be unable to eat. Even forcing a sip of water was difficult. She knew the altitude had come for her, and took an extra pill that day and allowed her dad and the boys to wait on her. They brought her cushions and toast and cool towels. She did not remember ever being treated so well. At home, she cared for everyone when they were sick. When she herself was ill, which was not often, she swallowed Pepto-Bismol or Dimetapp, sucked it up, and went on as usual. When her dad went to lie down in the evening, Aert and Bram argued over who would carry her to her room. Bram won, and his arms were firm, and warm and comforting. He laid her on the cot as gently as if she were a child and when he left Aert came in. He stood awkwardly by her bed for a moment, then bent down and kissed her lightly on the forehead with cool, dry lips that seemed to burn her. She smiled at him and closed her eyes, and when she opened them again, it was morning and he was gone.

The day of their ascent she felt much better: strong, happy and excited. At their breakfast of toast, margarine and jam, her dad talked excitedly to her and Jesse. She looked for the boys. Milan, noticing, handed her a folded note. They had left when the sun came up, and would wait for her and James at base camp. She felt a small wrinkle of disappointment which quickly faded under the day's preparations. They loaded their day packs with water, down jackets, ponchos, sunscreen, and chocolate bars. They dressed in layers and smeared Vaseline and sunscreen in a thick film on their lips. Trekking poles looped lightly around wrists, they set out. Everything, the last two weeks, the months of preparation, the books and dreams and plans, had all been for this day. The day they would stand at the base of the greatest mountain on earth.

The morning was overcast, and yet the sun was an intense, blistering, blinding presence. There was nothing living in this place. They were surrounded on all sides by impassable mountains, and the prolonged boom of thunder, which was the sound of avalanche. Each time they looked, their hearts skipping, thumping rapidly, they saw snow cascade waterfall-like down a mountain side. They said quiet prayers, thankful for the firm feel of rock beneath their boots.

It took six hours for them to reach the mountain. Six hours that could have been six days or six seconds; there was no time in this place. The base was a perfect replica of every picture she had studied, like stepping into one, like greeting an old, well-loved pen-pal for the first time. Margot dropped to her knees and placed both palms on the cold rock, removing her gloves to feel it with her bare skin. They placed their flag among the dozens of others strewn about the foot of the mountain, and snapped a picture. They looked for Aert and Bram, but they were not there. Margot felt a nagging worry, but when she saw that James was shivering, she forgot everything else in her concern for him. She too was shivering, despite the warmth of the sun, and she knew it was an effect, again, of the altitude. Their bodies, like a lizard's, were not able to regulate themselves without proper oxygen. They wanted both to stay there and to go, an odd mixture in equal proportions. To stay because it seemed they should, that they should linger here for as long as possible, that, perhaps they should never leave. To go, because their bodies screamed that they must. Finally, after only half an hour, they began their trek back down.

Every day, Margot looked for the boys. Every day, she asked at the next tea house if there was a note, or she checked the wall strewn with small papers for something from them, but there was only the usual: notes of encouragement, lists of names, Bible-verses, and mantras. They took a new route for their descent, an open, green, windswept route where they passed fields of sheep and goat and small, warm, chimneyed houses. But nowhere did she see the golden head of Aert or the black one of Bram. She fretted some, but was able to focus the bulk of her worry on James, whose knee ached almost as much and as consistently as Jesse's. Jesse gave him a vial of codeine and James seemed to be swallowing a small, white pill with every sip of water. They went slowly, one foot in front of the next, James leaning heavily on his trekking poles, like crutches, but Margot could see the lines of pain etched in his forehead and in his glazed eyes.

Soon the air became thick, heavy with oxygen, and this gave them strength for the remaining days. Still, Margot looked for the boys, but the closer they came to the origin of their trip the more thoughts of them were replaced with a dull longing for her children and her husband. Aert and Bram seemed like a dream. The entire two weeks seemed to fade and dissolve as rapidly as even the most vivid dream does upon waking. The two weeks up took them only five days down, and as they descended, the clouds that had been sparse fragments of white in an unspeakably blue sky began to descend with them, closing rapidly around them until every morning they awoke folded in a blanket of cloud. Usually, it cleared away by mid-afternoon, but the last day, the day they were supposed to leave, it did not. The small airplane that would take them back to Kathmandu and on to the United States could not fly. One day turned into two and two into five, and still the plane was grounded. They spent their days playing cards, drinking tea, reading. Margot found a copy of *Pilgrim's Progress* but could not get past the first few pages. Her mind wandered again and again to the window, to the sky beyond, looking for a break in the clouds. Sometimes one would come, teasing them, and they would watch anxiously, alerting Milan. She watched as a patch of blue appeared and then slowly closed as the grey cloud seemed to gradually encroach and then devour it.

On the fifth day Margot began to talk of hiking the rest of the way to Kathmandu. The rain had begun, beating through each night and barely subsiding with the morning. It seemed that the monsoon had arrived early, and from everything she had read, it was possible that no plane would get in or out for months. She felt desperate now, unable to think of anything but the soft arms of the baby and the feel of her husband's broad back and warm neck. James was worried; her state of mind seemed fragile. She woke each day with blood shot and dark-ringed eyes, she spoke to no one and often sat at a table in the tea house with her head in her hands, doing nothing. So, James agreed and Milan conceded that they would wait one more day, and then would head down. On the day they planned to go, there was another break in the cloud cover, larger than they had seen, a glorious patch of blue that shone and stayed. A helicopter was able to get through and was waiting for them in a field a mile away. Milan told them they would have to run to make it within a quarter of an hour. They pulled on their boots, stuffed their sleeping bags into their packs, and ran down the side of the mountain, charging through the undergrowth like a pack of wolves at the chase.

Margot could tell her dad's knee was torturing him but she did not care. All she could see was the patch of blue before her, and the clouds that seemed to gain on it every moment. She went back, several times, and grabbed both James and Jesse by the arms and dragged them with her own small weight and her great force of will. She ordered them to stop talking, and do nothing but run. Milan's hiking boots were ruined and he had only thin sandals which broke as they were crossing a stream. Margot grabbed the one that floated in the water and threw it and Milan, giving her only a single, wary look, proceeded without them.

When they emerged into the clearing, the pilot was standing, sweating, beneath what was now only a narrow oval of blue, barely big enough for the helicopter. Without a word to him, they jumped aboard and he took off, ascending into the opening just as the clouds converged. But they were free. Above and to either side of them was only blue, and beneath them stretched an endless sea of gray-white cloud.

They flew for several hours over vast expanses of undulating red earth, past mountains and forest and river and stream and Margot felt a measureless relief as she thought that they had nearly begun to descend this seemingly endless and infinitely harsh terrain on foot.

That night they stayed at the same hotel as when

they had first arrived, but now it felt plush and elegant and foreign. They took hot showers and slept again in cool white sheets, and the past two weeks faded further into dream with each passing hour.

Still, the day they left, she found herself looking, one last time for the open, friendly, stubbled face of Aert or the dark, somber, comforting one of Bram. But they were not there. As she and James stepped onto the plane, she took one final look behind her, and for a moment she thought she saw a blond head, a familiar smile, and two clear blue eyes that locked on hers. Then the crowd shifted, and the face was gone.

After thirty hours, and two stops, they arrived at the St Louis Airport. When the children saw her, for a moment, they seemed not to know what to do, then they all began talking and crying and hugging her at once. She folded them in her arms as best she could and looking up, found the warm, brown eyes of her husband waiting to lock on her own. He stepped towards her, and the children, sensing him there, opened a space for him. He wrapped her in his arms and she rested her head against his chest just below the line of his collar bone where she felt the pulse of his heart. He kissed the top of her head, and she felt the last bit of the dream dissolve beneath her feet, until there was only the dull haze of a St Louis sun reflected on black asphalt, and a minivan waiting to take her home.

3. THE HOUSEWIFE'S HANDYMAN

Pete Sauer would be thirty-six on Tuesday. Thirty-six. That meant he was closer to forty than thirty. Just four more years to do everything he had set out to. Four more years to make his life, not exactly meaningful, but at least memorable. He scratched at the week-old growth sprouting from his chin and jaw line. He never did like having a beard. He didn't care if it made him look older, as Cora had told him. He didn't have to do what she said. He would shave it in the morning. Better anyway, not to have extra hair to leave around. Cora was his seventy three year-old mother. She was a hideous person. A face like a shriveled pumpkin, with small sunken black eyes, stringy gray hair, a thin, angry, purple mouth. She stunk of stale perfume and baby powder. They had one thing in common: a mutual dislike for one another. They lived in a small, bright apartment downtown. They moved here shortly after he turned fifteen, for a fresh start. Or an escape.

Through the window a park was visible. A beautiful park of gnarled oak, ginkgo, magnolia. In the spring it bloomed with pastel-hued tulip and cheerful buttery daffodil. In summer the small pond was covered in water lilies and couples sat entwined in the shade of leafy sycamores. Pete only spent the summers here now, needing to stay on the move. His predilection for certain things that less imaginative people found distasteful was hindering him. Hindering him from moving forward with life. As a brooding teen, watching the transformation in seasons from his bedroom window, especially from the dark-dead of winter to the bright fresh spring, had made him think change could be possible, even in him.

But Pete Sauer knew he was not this place. There was nothing that opened up in him revealing a garden hidden beneath the winter frost. Beneath the small dark exterior, there was nothing delightful waiting. Oh, there were things to be discovered, for sure. Most people just didn't think they were very pleasant things. Perhaps, if, during his formative years, he had been blessed with parents who believed in him, who cared about him, a father who didn't continuously point out his faults and his probability of ending up in juvey, a mother who didn't look at him with revulsion and mistrust. Well, maybe things would have been different. Or maybe not.

Pete began working as a handyman right out of high school. He never considered college. He knew it was a bunch of BS. A load of pretentious presidential hopefuls, all patting each other on the back and lauding their own accomplishments. Reading useless shit and thanking each other for the pleasure. Half of them would likely end up as management for the local Home Depot or teaching first graders how to wipe their asses. No thanks. Pete knew he wanted something a bit more, well, exciting. The only thing college had going for it, as he saw it, was the girls. And handymen saw plenty of those too. His uncle Mitt, who started him out in the business, told him all about it. The desperate little housewives whose only adult contact was their lawn-boy, their pool-boy, or their handyman. They were ripe for the picking. Or so said Uncle Mitt. Pete's experience, at least in the beginning, was not quite all that.

"Pee-to" his father would call in his heavy German accent, waving erratically from the window of the Chevy, as Pete tried to dash into school unseen. His father didn't understand the connotation—*pedo*, short for pedophile. The other kids, of course, enjoyed it immensely. Or maybe his father did understand. Pete had wondered about that too, on occasion. It would have been just like him, knowing what it meant, having his own little joke at the expense of his son. Reasoning to himself that he was toughening the little sissy up. Yeah, that would be just like him.

Pete was no sissy though, and never had been. Sure, he wasn't a big guy and maybe had been called small at some now forgotten point in his life, but that never deterred him. He could make a bloody mess of a kid twice his size at the ripe age of nine. It was all in the mind. Mind games: that's what he was good at. If you could intimidate someone, making them think you were scarier, crazier, faster, stronger, then you had power over them. It didn't matter if you were actually any of those things or not. You just had to seem like it. Pete would have been a great actor.

Free will. It's what sets us apart from the beasts, makes us godlike. Pete knew this. He knew that each day he made a multitude of decisions that directed his life, and one decision led to the next in an endless series. Barely into adolescence, Pete did three things that would send his life spiraling down a dark and endless path. Two were accidents, one was not. They all happened in a rapid succession that spanned three years. Three years that would define the next twenty.

When he was twelve his mother became pregnant. His parents were ecstatic. His mother was nearing the end of her child-bearing years and they didn't think they would have any more. At first, Pete was unsure of his feelings as he watched his mother's belly swell beneath the thin white t-shirts and long black skirts. She was tired and even more impatient with him, protective of the small life she was growing. He often found her sitting, alone, on the couch in a sunny spot, rubbing her ripe belly, singing softly. He had no memory of her ever singing to him, but wondered jealously if she had. Each day this jealousy expanded in him, consuming his small heart. Once he found himself standing over her in the dark, holding a kitchen knife. He slunk back to bed, shaking at the thought of what his father would have done if he had seen him. One day, he went to hug her and she shoved him roughly away and told him not to touch her, circling her arms around her belly defensively. That afternoon, as she stood on the top of the stairs, he thought of pushing her, not to hurt her, but to get rid of the thing that had taken any little bit of affection she had ever felt for him. So, then, when she was six months along and went into early labor and lost the baby, he knew he was the one that had wished that into existence. In a cruel fit, his mother made him come and look at the tiny, purple, shriveled, repulsive body of his sister. He found himself crying, something he did not remember doing before or since.

When he was thirteen, there was an accident. His father, as usual, picked him up from school in the Chevy Suburban. That hunter-green Chevy his mother had won in a sweepstakes four years before. Pete hated it. Not just the color, but the car itself and everything it stood for. They could never have afforded to buy it and everyone knew it. The other children and neighbors laughed at them, mostly behind their backs. Sometimes to their faces. More than once Pete wished he could get someone to steal the fucking thing. Then he could just walk to school like the rest of the kids. Pete, though, always self-sufficient, had a plan. Not to have the car stolen, that was too mundane, plus he didn't really have any friend he'd trust enough or was savvy enough for the job. No: blowing it up, that was the thing to do. He replaced the car's gas line with one that went straight to the tank. This model had, stupidly, been built without a fuel pump, so a small fire in the engine could easily back up into the gas tank. Pete put a tiny hole in the fuel line, near the carburetor. His plan was to allow some gas to leak onto the engine. He would ignite it using a disconnected spark-plug wire. It would take a minute for the spark to reach the tank, giving him just enough time to make a run for it.

It was Saturday morning and his parents were still sleeping, or fooling around, when he set it. The car was parked in the usual place: on the street, by the sidewalk in front of the house. Pete was crouched behind the overgrown holly bushes on the small grassy spot opposite the sidewalk. He watched, feeling like he was at a movie, fascinated and horrified all at once, but completely incapable of doing anything, as his father came down the front steps and got into the car. The explosion was more powerful than Pete had anticipated and there was a cloud of smoke and a sort of after-shock so strong that it rippled through the sidewalk, cracking it, like a small earthquake had erupted and turned it, for a moment, to liquid. Bits of iron, glass and rubber hurtled through the air, combined with bits of his father. One piece of hunter-green metal that had pulled lose from the top of the passenger door lodged itself in Pete's arm, just below the shoulder. Even after it was removed, stitched, and had healed, he could feel where the metal had embedded itself and sometimes his arm jerked suddenly like it was remembering and trying to move out of the way. And when the weather was just right, rainy or misty or humid, it ached.

Most everyone believed it was an accident, especially since, unbeknownst to Pete, and as luck would have it, there had been a recall on this particular model because of two instances of exploding gas tanks. They ended up with enough money from the lawsuit to get them through the next few years. Pete got a sort of grim satisfaction from fooling everyone. When the nightmares came and he awoke clutching at the lurching snake of fear in his stomach, he tried to tell himself his father deserved it, and was the biggest fool of all.

The third thing Pete did was one year later. He was fourteen now, with all the hormones and angst that inevitably brought. Repulsed by his antics at school and suspicious of everything he did, his mother had distanced herself.

Her best friend, Marge, whose husband had left a few years before, asked if her daughter could stay at their house for the weekend. She had breast cancer and her double mastectomy was scheduled for Friday. She'd be in the hospital until Monday. Cora had a long conversation with Pete before she said yes. "Pete," she said in her preachy, wheedling mom's voice, "the Jones are going through a lot right now. Marge really needs our help. She needs us to watch her little girl for the weekend. I know it's been pretty rough since—" Here she paused, looking at him hard, knowing it gave Pete the shivers. He wanted so bad to slap her when she looked like that." —since the accident—" She emphasized the word 'accident', *way to be obtuse, ma,* he thought. "I want you to be good. Do you hear me? Real good. Maybe just stay out of the way. You're not to go near that little girl unless it's to be like a big brother to her."

"Sure, ma," Pete said, giving her his most charming smile, but inwardly boiling at the accusation she hadn't quite leveled, "whatever you say."

Pete knew what people thought of him. He could feel the deep mistrust and dislike boiling beneath the surface of his own mother's thinly veiled tolerance. Her friends hardly came over, and they squinted at him or looked at him from the corners of their eyes, never head on. As if he were a rabid dog that might leap at them any moment. He could only imagine what the bitch told them over coffee. That he was always in the bathroom masturbating to his filthy pictures? That he watched dirty videos and cursed at her and left fingerprints on her arm when she turned off the internet? That he walked in his sleep and once she found him standing in the living room holding a knife to his own throat? After that she had taken to locking the knives in the bedroom with her at night. He knew it was not because she worried he would harm himself.

Pete waited until Sunday. Waiting was hard. That little girl, she was eight or nine, so not all that little, he thought, laid in the room next to his all night Saturday, in her thin white nightgown, with her thin white legs and her little breasts. Pete's heart pounded and he barely slept. Sunday night he waited just long enough to be sure his mother was asleep, then he went in. He didn't do much, just moved himself back and forth on her, kissed her so she couldn't scream. His shoulder ached from having to hold her down and he cursed her for hurting him, told her he would kill her and her whole family if she told, made sure she believed it. He was sick with revulsion for days, and the next few times he got girls at school behind the bleachers or in the locker and held them against their will, he was sick too. But each time was a little less, and his appetite for these violent encounters, or the power they gave him, only grew.

The housewives fought a bit more than the girl had, but that was part of the fun. And he was strong now, much stronger than any of them. There were only two small problems. One was keeping them quiet. The other problem was his shoulder, which had begun to bother him almost constantly, and hurt nearly to the point of tears when he had to strain to hold them down, at the same time keeping his hand over their mouths, stifling their liquid, gurgling, or hysterical screams. The funny thing was, he never associated the pain with the car accident. *Fuck the girl,* he found himself thinking again and again as the pain shot through his arm, *fuck the goddamned girl.*

The housewives, or stay-at-home-moms (whatever you wanted to call them), were all stupid. He was just giving them what they wanted. They were so thrilled when he showed up, young, handsome, tan and muscled. He could almost see them salivating. He knew they all fantasized about it in their dreary little houses while they watched re-runs of Friends or the Ellen show. Funny thing, when they finally got what they had been day-dreaming about, none of them really seemed to want it after all. Except once, and he found that was a real turn-off. He was careful, made it hard enough to trace him that no-one had gotten close to catching him yet. It was fun, too, outsmarting all those educated detective pricks, all those baby-faced police officers, and the prissy housewives too. He had perfected his acting skills on them, perfected the artistic form known as seduction. Still, he was cautious, and moved, often. He was only living with his mother temporarily; it was nice, though, to have a home base. Pretty soon, he'd probably move again. After the next job. Or maybe the one after that.

***

Anna and John had rented a sizeable brownstone in the city. They had moved there just after John finished his MD/PhD at SUNY Upstate. From the street it looked small, being one of those narrow row houses with mere feet separating it from the homes on either side. But you only had to look up to see its size.

Most people didn't look up.

It was also deceptive on the inside. The first floor seemed dark and closed in— cave-like since there were only windows on one side and those opened to the neighbor's red brick walls. But if you stayed long enough to be given a tour, or ventured on your own up the long front stairway, you would be pleasantly surprised by the second floor. This opened into a different house entirely, filled with a startling amount of light, with soaring ceilings, stained glass windows and picturesque reading nooks. Here, too, you could see that the home was quite large as it continued up a second flight of stairs to a third, even more charmingly bright and open attic-like apartment.

Anna loved this house. Perhaps because it was a bit like her. Small and unassuming from the front, hardly even noticeable, but opening up to reveal something quite different within.

Anna was exhausted. Nearly eight months pregnant in the middle of the St Louis summer. It was a special kind of hell. John was in his first year of residency at Barnes Jewish Hospital. The home they had found was just a five-minute drive from work. That was a blessing. In so many cities you had to commute an hour or more. Then she would really never see him. Most of their family was in upstate New York where John had gone to medical school and completed his PhD in neurology and Anna had completed her teacher training. She was on her own for the first time. At the start, she had been excited. Finally, they were venturing out, grown-ups for real. Then she got pregnant right after their move, and she just wanted to go home. She wanted to stop in and see her mom, she wanted a cup of tea and someone with a sympathetic ear to listen to her complaints and tell her it would all be okay. It didn't help that John was hardly ever around, living his own brand of hell as a first-year internal medicine resident. When he finally did come home, after a 12, maybe 18-hour shift, the last thing he wanted to do was listen to her groan about the heat and how many pounds she had gained that week. But St Louis wasn't all bad. Despite her family's misgivings over the high crime rate, she had found it a welcoming and vibrant community. The house was within walking distance of the zoo, an art museum, a science center, and a beautiful park full of meandering trails, large grassy spaces, and sparkling fountains. She thought what fun it would be to take the baby to all these places once he was old enough. That made her smile. She was going to be a mom. What a strange and wonderful thing.

She and John had decided together that she would not look for a teaching job right away, allowing them time to settle into their new home first, and settle into life with a baby. Maybe, after the first year, she would want to start looking. She didn't know. Although she felt restless, not working or studying for the first time in her life, it was also a free sort of feeling. Her days were her own. No one to tell her what to do or where to go. Each day held a new beginning full of possibility. Probably, for some people, the lack of routine or organization would be overwhelming, but it made Anna giddy. She had always felt stifled by other people's expectations of her, their endless need to turn her into what they thought she should be. The gnawing desire to please them, that she often hated herself for. She had her own demons, and maybe, during this time of restlessness, she could face them.

They were married during college, being both from Christian homes that frowned on living together. So, by the time they graduated they had already been married two years and felt they were ready to have children. Looking back, it was very naïve of them. She was 21, he 22, there was really no hurry. But they were both the kind of people that wanted life to move along. For Anna, it was about filling that frightening, empty place in her. A place of dark memory and hungry desire, with something cleaner, brighter. A baby, she felt sure, would do that. But month upon month passed until their sum was a year, and still no baby. They went together to the doctor and were told that she had something called diminished ovarian reserve, basically, a shockingly low supply of viable eggs. "It is very good," the fertility specialist said in his heavy Greek accent, looking Anna up and down in a way that made her feel undressed, exposed and scrutinized all at once, "that you are starting this early. In a few more years, maybe three, you would most likely not be able to get pregnant at all, at least with your own eggs." They used in vitro. It was terrible.

Anna never got used to the needles and usually

locked herself in the bathroom so John couldn't see her cry as she lifted her shirt, pinched the soft skin of her belly between two fingers, took a deep shaky breath, and inserted the long thin line of it in the fold. Finally, after nearly eight excruciating years of needles, hormones, surgical egg extractions, the loss of two viable pregnancies, the endless waiting and waiting to do it all again…it looked like they would have their baby. Of course, they both lived in constant fear that something would go wrong. And instead of that fear dissipating a bit the further the pregnancy went, it only increased until it was difficult to think of anything else. Sometimes Anna found herself in a horrible daydream, where every scenario of loss went through her mind. What if she went in and there was no heartbeat, as had happened in the fourth month of her second pregnancy? Would she be able to hold it together? Would she go crazy? What would she tell John? Would she call him at work or wait until he was home and in her arms? She hid these fears from him, knowing he had his own. Fearing, too, that to speak them aloud would be to speak them into existence.

***

It was a bright, nearly cloudless summer morning. Still early enough that the sun had not burned off the cool of the night. Anna went out to the porch with a cup of lukewarm coffee. John always made her a cup before he went to work, even if it was only 5 AM when he left. His small gesture of love. If he ever stopped she would know something was terribly wrong. She smiled at that. What could ever be wrong? Today, everything was perfect. It was John's birthday and she had planned a surprise. She had sold a few odds and ends over the past few weeks on Marketplace and Craigslist, a blue bench which she had found and painted when they were first married, an old bicycle that needed the rust cleaned off, a pile of her clothes. She had made enough to buy them a nice TV. The one they currently owned was only fourteen inches: she didn't even think they made them that small anymore. The new one was a thirty-six inch mammoth. John's passion, when he had the time for passions, was football. He didn't quite complain but sometimes bemoaned the poor quality of the picture which seemed to lengthen out at the edges of the TV screen, and more recently, the small crack in the left corner with web-like tendrils protruding out from its center, which was impossible to avoid looking at. John would love her gift.

She had typed 'handyman in my area' into her phone a couple of days ago and called the first name that popped up. A Brian Appleman of Appleman's Handy Services. He was booked until late July. The second man would not do such a small job. "Ma'am, if you ever need an addition or a bathroom remodel, I'm your man." She politely said goodbye and tried the third number. A man answered on the first ring.

"Hello," said the voice on the other end. It was a young voice. Anna hesitated for a moment, but only just.

"Hi," she answered, brightly, "I'm trying to get someone to hang a TV for me. No, I mean, mount a TV. Yes, that's it. It's for my husband's birthday, which is in two days. I've already talked to two other guys and they couldn't do it. I'm really hoping you might be able to help me?" She sounded ridiculous to herself. Pleading and babbling at once, like a desperate little girl. Like a moron.

"Sure," the voice said, "No problem at all. I can come tomorrow. Just give me your address. How's about ten sound?"

"That's great. Perfect.Thanks so much. I really do appreciate it. You have no idea." She was babbling again, recognized it, hastily gave him her address and hung up. She realized too late that she had forgotten to ask his name. The info on her phone just said "The Housewife's Handyman". Oh well, she thought, she could ask him when he came.

Anna had never hired a handyman before; she had never had the money or the need. When they lived in New York her stepdad would stop by once a week to fix anything that needed it. Now, while John was learning how to diagnose a stroke or intubate a patient who couldn't breathe on their own, she was learning how to keep their home from falling apart. It made her feel useful and mostly she enjoyed it. It was incredible what you could figure out how to do watching videos on YouTube. She had repaired their dishwasher, refrigerator and vacuum cleaner all this way. She would have hung the TV herself too, but in her current state the television was too hard to lift on her own.

By 9 a.m. it was already too hot to be outdoors. She would have loved to go for a walk but merely stepping out the front door started the sweat pouring from her hairline to her thighs. She had pulled her hair up, off her neck, and wore a light cream-colored cotton dress. She had never worn dresses much until becoming pregnant. Now, she could hardly stand anything else. Even shorts clung to her legs and pressed on her stomach in all the wrong places. She spent most of the morning doing chores, laundry, dishes, bills, all the usual. Then, at nine-thirty she pulled the TV into the living room from its hiding spot under a blanket in the hall closet. She thought maybe she could help the handyman so she opened the mounting kit and laid the pieces out with the instructions next to them. Then, second-guessing herself, she put them all neatly back in the box again, taping it firmly shut. Exactly at ten o'clock, the doorbell rang.

She answered it to find a man a few years older than her, clean-shaven with a thick crop of dark hair. He was the kind of man that wanted to be noticed, the kind with eyes that said, I know you want to look, so go ahead and look. She didn't like it. She also didn't like the way he seemed to look her up and down, slowly, without even trying to seem like he was doing something else. When he got to her bulging stomach, he paused for a moment and she shivered. She thought, for an instant, of telling him he had the wrong address, but then she remembered the TV, and that today was John's birthday. So instead, she opened the door and led him into the living room.

"That's where you want it?" He said, gesturing at the wall above the brick fireplace.

"Yes, if you can."

"Oh, I can. I can put it just about anywhere you like." He looked at her again, long enough to make her discomfort grow. She wanted to look away.

"There will be fine. Thank you." She would just keep this professional, she thought, a half hour tops, and he'd be gone. She had to stop imagining such ridiculous things. But there was something about him. Something familiar. the way his eyes drifted back and forth over her, over the room, over everything really. Like they were restless, or looking for something.

"Well, once I put it there, there's no going back. Not without a lot of extra work anyway. If you change your mind, the wall will have to be patched and painted otherwise you'll have a gaping hole right over your fireplace. So just be real sure, that's all." She found herself studying his face as he talked. She had opened the blinds on the one large front window and there was a play of summer sun and shadow on his face that seemed to make it alter constantly. And yet, she couldn't shake the feeling of familiarity.

"That's where I want it. I'm sure. How long do you think it'll take? I might just go lie down for a bit until you're done."

"Oh, half an hour, maybe forty-five minutes, tops. You go right ahead and take yourself a nap. I'm sure that little creature inside of you just sucks all the energy, doesn't it?"

She nodded, trying to smile. She made her way upstairs. But she did not go into the room she shared with John. Instead, she found herself in the nursery. It was a small, cheerful room, painted a soft tapioca yellow. In one corner was what amounted to a broom closet, suitable only for tiny baby things. Opposite was an enormous bay window, a window that took up nearly one entire wall. The light streamed in long lines across the floor, over the crib and the wooden rocker that Anna sat in. She had no intention of napping. She had needed to get out of there. This room was as far removed from the dark lower floor as the sky was from the earth's center. There was something, a terrible something, scratching at the back of her mind, clawing to get out. But it kept slipping away before she could get her fingers into it. She sat, rocking gently, and closed her eyes. There it was, a feeling, like a word you can't think of but are sure you know. It was there, she just couldn't quite grasp it.

When she awoke, the first thing she saw was a shadow in the doorway, framed by a halo of morning light. She did not feel afraid, merely confused. Was John home early? Then, she remembered. The man had a faraway look, cold and distant, like someone who was not present.

"Is it finished?" she asked, praying the hesitation didn't show in her voice. He didn't answer for a moment. Only continued, in the same manner, staring at something not there. Finally, just as she was ready to repeat the question, he shuddered and seemed to see her.

"Hmmm? Oh, yes. Yes. You should come and see." His voice was soft and Anna wondered at the change in his demeanor. Instead of putting her at ease, she felt a sudden sick fear shiver through her. She shoved it down and heaved herself out of the rocker. One leg had gone numb and it took her a moment before she could put weight on it. He didn't look away, but watched her. The image that flitted through her mind: cat and mouse.

Down the stairs, he walked close enough that she could hear the whisper of his jeans and feel hot breath on her neck. With difficulty she kept her pace even. Everything in her wanted to run.

"It looks good" She said "Thank you. What do I owe you?"

"It's thirty for a full hour, but I'll just charge you twenty-five, since it wasn't quite that."

"Thirty's fine" she said, not wanting to feel indebted to this man.

"All right," he said, walking towards her slowly and taking the money. His fingers brushed hers, a soft cold touch of flesh against flesh, and she shivered for the second time. She wanted him to go. But he didn't. "There's something's been bothering me since I got here. You look so familiar. And I don't think you ever gave me your name. Maybe it happens we've met before. Wouldn't that be a funny coincidence."

Hardly, Anna thought, and then, for some reason she gave him a name that was not hers. "No," he said, "No, no, never knew any Pamela Bright. Never knew a Pamela at all, married or not, and I never forget a name. Must've just been someone that looked like you."

Still, that terrible wariness pulled at her mind, a memory that would not come. She swallowed it down and walked him to the door.

"Goodbye, thank you again."

"Bye now," he said, turning toward her on the threshold. He gave her a long look that stopped on her belly. His eyes were dark, almost completely taken up with the pupil that had dilated in the dim hall. He licked his lips, turned, and walked down the five cement steps that led to the sidewalk. He was holding his shoulder, and she wondered if he had hurt it hanging the TV. She could just make out the words he mumbled to himself as he turned, massaging the shoulder" *fuck the girl.*"

In that instant, she remembered. She closed the door with a sharp click behind him, fastening all three bolts and leaned against it, the sweat pouring off of her forehead, into her eyes, heart racing, nausea rising. She closed her eyes, forcing her breath to slow.

She placed both hands on her belly, and felt the baby kick.

4. A CHILD IN THE WINDOW

Lena had all her shots and a vial of malaria pills. She was 16 and was going to Africa. The boy she loved was going too. A blonde, burly, blue-eyed, guitar-playing, poetry-writing, Bible-loving, med-school-bound boy. Tonight, she lay in her twin bed, the heavy purple and violet plaid cover pulled to her chin. She stared at the edge of the window where the dark sky was visible, starless, silky and black. Her eyes were heavy and she felt the weight of sleep pulling on her. It was in this half-state that she saw a pale girl's face in the window. Her groggy mind worked slowly. It took her too long to realize the impossibility of the face, three floors up, where there were no stairs from the outside. When the absurdity of the image clicked, she sat upright, rubbed at her eyes and opened them again, wider, as if the gesture would revive reality. But the girl was still there. Lena stared at her, finding that if she looked hard, the girl's face became distorted. She had to look from the corner of her eye, or to the side of the image. Then she could see that it was dark where the eyes should be as if they opened onto the sky behind. The face was ethereal, so pale it almost glowed and the hair was wispy and white. The small, pink mouth smiled: a sweet, little-girl smile. It was unmistakably the face of a child, no more than five or six. Lena was a practical person, not taken to flights of fancy, though she loved the idea of them, the drama and poetry of others'flightiness. She herself would never imagine something that was not there.

She tried to think. She knew she should feel afraid. Instead, she felt only a keen fascination. She rubbed her eyes for a second time, stretched her limbs, and turned around once. When she opened them and faced the window again, the girl was still there. She stood in front of the bed, where the face was centered and nearly level with her own and did a mental run-through of the day. It was Saturday, so she did not go to school. Her mother had taken her for a haircut in the morning. Lena had insisted on cutting her long, heavy, dark curls to her chin. Short hair was the most practical thing. Africa would be hot, and many of the children at the orphanage would have lice. Short hair was cooler, easier to manage, and less prone to an infestation. But despite all her reasons, she had cried when they finished and she saw herself in the mirror. Her mother, of course, could not let well enough alone, and had to remind Lena that she told her not to do it. She didn't cry because she really cared about the hair, she cried because she thought the boy she loved might have. After this, her mother had taken her to lunch, *to soften the hair incident and have some quality mother-daughter bonding time, since you'll be leaving me soon*—her exact words. Lena would never understand why mothers had to talk like this, but they all did. Every single mother in all of history talked in exactly the same way.

Lena tried to re-focus, realizing that her mind was wandering. She repeatedly tried to focus directly on the face, but, again, it blurred and shifted, became blurry, as if she had removed her glasses or was looking at one of those 3-D optical illusions. She shoved her hands in the pockets of her sweatpants. She circled her fingers around the rim of a small, smooth vial, only then remembering about the malaria pills.

***

With his seemingly endless supply of energy, Paul had left with the kids for the ferry almost two hours ago. He was on call that weekend, but things at the clinic were slow and it was unlikely he'd need to go in. Lena had no desire to go. Not in this heat. The heat was like a paper bag shoved over the head, suffocating, causing every pore in the body to open and release a torrent of sweat. Missouri was not a nice place in the summer. Lena did feel a tiny bit guilty. Faking a headache to have some time to herself was a low thing to do. She had pictured an afternoon binge-watching something sleazy and drinking mimosas but hadn't yet moved from the bed where she was alternating between scanning Facebook posts and deleting junk mail. What a pile of crap her life had become. If she taught her kids one thing, it would be to not end up like her. Paul, of course, would say she was being ungrateful. And he would be right. But she couldn't help it. Yes, of course, she had chosen to get married at only eighteen, to start with children a few months after, to forgo college and a career in order to raise the children. She had a good life, a happy, perfectly satisfactory life, by any account. But if she could go back, she might not make the same choices, at least not in the same order. Lena put down her phone and drifted off into a peaceful sleep (the kind born of the absence of children fighting, and the coolness of air conditioning), when the phone rang.

***

South Africa was spectacular. Everything more alive. Lena felt as if her life was a black and white film before, and now it was full color. That's how she described it to her mother. But it was more than that. The colors were more vivid, greens greener, the blue sky bluer, and everything tasted full of life, smelled full of life. Nothing was distilled, diluted, or genetically modified. It was real. The people too. Passionate, loud, unafraid. They spent two days in this place, visiting the Cape of Good Hope and Table Rock Mountain and the prison cell of Nelson Mandela. They ogled, and spoke in hushed, awed voices. She had her first beer, ordered in full view of the adults, since the drinking age was sixteen. She never wanted to leave.

***

Then they went to Mozambique. They should have done it the other way around. She understood continent and country. There were never two places more dissimilar. The colors faded to two: earth-brown and sand. The tastes were three: hard sharp cheese, hard glutenous bread, oily fish. At the orphanage, where they went to work, she was surrounded by children, and this added another layer, because they were not joyful and carefree like children at home. They were drained of life, wary and frightened. Like old men and women trapped in children's bodies. Lena cried there twice: on the first day and on the last.

On the airplane she told the boy she loved about the

vision of the girl in her bedroom. He laughed and said, *of course it was a hallucination induced by the Malaria pills, you didn't drink enough water when you took them.* She already knew this, and yet—in Mozambique, she looked for the girl.

She found her in the small, shriveled face of a baby.

Each day the team went to the local dump. The dump was where they found children to bring back to the orphanage. The children were without parents, either because their parents had died in the civil war, had been killed by a forgotten land mine, or had simply and quietly abandoned them there. In the dump there was food. The children raced behind the garbage truck and fought over the choicest morsels. Half a rotten banana, a bag of molded bread, an apple with only a few bites taken and no worms. The children barely had clothes and none had shoes. They were stringy, except for their bulging bellies, and tough like leather. In the dump they were crafty and cunning, without time or energy for children's games or children's ways. Lena and the boy she loved were together when they found the baby. He almost stepped on it. It was buried in the garbage, tucked in as if its mother had laid it there for the night, covered in black flies. They dug away the steaming garbage and pulled it out. Lena thought it was dead, but then it let out a small whimpering breath. Its eyes were caked shut and it was sickeningly thin. Unimaginably thin. It looked old and frail and not really like a baby at all. And its hair was white as well as the sparse eyebrows and lashes, were white. Lena wrapped it in her head scarf and they carried it back to the orphanage.

For the next three weeks they sat with the baby. They took turns holding her, feeding her milk with a medicine dropper, like a kitten, then later with a bottle. It turned out she was actually a toddler, two, possibly three years old but with the body of a six-month old. The boy played his guitar and Lena sang. 'If you're happy and you know it,' 'Jesus Loves Me,' 'The Wheels on the Bus.' Lena bathed her and kissed her and often slept in the sunshine with the baby nestled against her breast. In three weeks the baby could not be recognized as the same one they had found buried in the dump. She could sit up on her own and would play with small rocks or twigs, humming bits of the songs they sung to her. The boy built her stick houses and taught her words which she cooed out in a high cheerful voice. Lena asked the director about her pale hair, and her eyes, which were a soft pink. She was an albino, a baby of luck. Lena and the boy fell in love with the baby, who the director named Venusha, and their feelings of love for her became intermixed with feelings of love for each other.

The day they left was an impossible day. Venusha clung to their necks and cried and the director had to pry her small fingers apart to get her away. She had not spent a day away from them in four weeks. Lena wept bitter, angry tears, because, at sixteen, she was not old enough to adopt a child. The boy and her sat hand in hand for nearly the entire fifteen hours on the airplane, feeling a small comfort in their joint sorrow. His name was Paul, and two years later, as soon as they were able, they married.

Lena wanted to go back for Venusha, but got pregnant with her own child only a few months after marriage. At first, hardly a day went by when she did not see the face of the little girl appearing again in her mind. But it faded gradually until it was only in her dreams. Dreams where she promised she would come back. She woke up slick with sweat and a cool, dark longing for the baby she would never have.

The phone rang for the third time before Lena managed to get up, a high tinkling bell sound. *Damn it*, she thought, *why didn't I turn the volume off? I'd never get back to sleep now*. She had placed the phone on the window ledge by the bed and rolled over, groaning as she reached for it. The voice that streamed out of it was soft and flat and cottony. Lena had to strain to hear what it said. "Is this Ms. Halbek?"

"Yes, this is she." Lena answered, irritably, propping herself on the pillows and wondering if she should just hang up rather than listen to the spiel on home security systems or direct TV, or whatever the voice would be trying to sell her.

"Are you sitting down?"

"Um, sure," said Lena, slightly bewildered.

"You were listed as the emergency contact for Paul Halbek, Michael Halbek, and Mary Halbek."

"The what?" Lena could hardly hear the voice on the other end and wanted to scream at her to speak up.

"The emergency contact for Paul Halbek, Michael Halbek, Mary Halbek," said the voice, only slightly louder this time.

"Yes, yes, I'm Paul's wife. Those are my kids. Why? What's going on?" Lena suddenly felt terror rise in her throat. What the hell did they need an emergency contact for? She swung her legs off the bed and stood up. "And can you please speak up, I can hardly hear a thing you're saying."

"I'm so sorry, Ms. Halbek," said the soft, cotton-filled voice, "but there has been an accident."

For the first week Lena left the news on continuously, as if doing this would either confirm reality or alter it. It did neither. She didn't cry because she didn't believe any of it. Her mother came to stay and tried once to switch off the television, Lena tore around the house like a madwoman looking for the remote, tearing her hair and mumbling incoherently until she switched it back on.

After a week, the live news coverage died down, replaced with other more recent, more pressing things, and so Lena spent hours poring through the footage captured by passengers on a nearby boat. Videos of a sunny, blue sky suddenly turning gray and then black, waves like the ocean and wind like a hurricane, and the small boat slowly sinking lower and lower in those waves, until it disappeared from sight. She tried so hard to see the faces of passengers in the windows, but they were only a blur through the torrential rain. Many of the passengers on the other boat, the luckier passengers, had been interviewed and lauded for their bravery and forethought in getting pictures and videos of the incident. But all Lena could think was, *why didn't they dive in? Why didn't they help? Didn't they know there were children?* She hated them. Every one of them.

At the end of six months, her mother took matters into her own hands. She bought Lena a one-way ticket to Mozambique. She had contacted the director at the orphanage, who, wonderfully, was the same one Lena had known almost fourteen years ago. He said that they would be thrilled to have her. Lena's mother packed her bags and drove her to the airport. Lena hardly knew what was happening. At security, her mother kissed her goodbye and tucked something small into the pocket of her jacket. On the plane, Lena remembered it and pulled it out. It was folded in half twice and Lena carefully unwrapped it. Two things fell out, one tucked inside the other. In the first she saw a sixteen-year-old girl, tan and freckled with a crop of short, dark curls, holding a pale, thin child. In the second, a girl stood alone, lean of face and body, in her late teens, with hair white as snow, eyelashes and eyebrows the same, a small smile playing at the corners of her mouth.

5. IN DEFENSE OF THE HARVEST

The idea for The Harvest is not new. Two weeks ago I read a story from a paper published in the early 2030s about a fourteen year-old boy named Daniel who was waiting for a heart transplant. He was biking to school when, WHAM, a UPS truck slammed into him, crushing him, breaking twenty-three bones and smashing his heart and lungs. Miraculously, he survived, though he was on life support and his family was living in fear that each day would be his last. The mother of the man whose heart was used in the transplant visited Daniel in the hospital. She held his hand and wept as she listened to her own son's heart beat again in this young man. The Harvest gave many mothers a second chance.

I had a feeling I would be getting a phone call but was still surprised when the voice on the other end was that deep, gravelly one the last twelve years have made us all so familiar with. "Mr. Lots. Mr. Eliazar Lots?" the voice said, "are you ready to do your duty as an American citizen? To protect and uphold the freedoms of your fellow countrymen? To come to the aid of your president?" Well, let me tell you, I'm a simple man, but I'm not too proud to admit these words stirred me to tears. Of course I was ready.

I am well aware of the current temperature of public opinion. My wife and I have been closely following the news. Especially the trial and more importantly the criminal defense attorney, who happens to be our daughter. We have not spoken in several years, not since she took up with the 'Last Harvesters' movement. This letter is as much to her as it is to all of you. A reminder of why The Harvest exists and of all it has done for the greater good. I have heard the rumors that politicians, lawmakers, and others are benefiting financially from The Harvest. I find, generally, that public scrutiny goes through phases. I have seen at least half a dozen of these in the past thirty-five years. Yet The Harvest remains. What is different about this trial is our daughter. As part of the first family to experience both tragedy and benefits from The Harvest, I am in a unique position to write on the topic.

As far as I know The Harvest in its current form was first put forth by a certain Dr. William D. Chomes, though I believe (based on my own research) that it was talked about in the medical community, especially among surgeons and physicians whose specific job was caring for the incarcerated, for many years before he wrote his polarizing paper on the topic. Dr. Chomes is now all but forgotten and it is, instead, Dr. Elizabeth Fortright, whose brother was a correctional officer murdered by an angry inmate with a blade hidden in his anal cavity, who brought public attention to Chomes' ideas.

Harvesting human organs from the dead to use in saving a life is a practice that had already been around for centuries and although there were still those who struggled with the idea (I remember my own grandfather telling me there was "no way in hell" he would let "any damn doctor" cut him up. If he ever ended up in a hospital, he'd "be good and sure they had no reason to end his life earlier than God had intended"), most people were reasonable enough to realize its extraordinary, almost miraculous, benefits. And the overwhelming number of stories of boys and girls being given a second chance at life were enough to shame any sceptics into silence.

My own Sadie was three when Dr. Fortright's ideas began to take shape in the public mind. There was a lot of buzz around what had happened to her brother, a lot of talk about her theories being based on revenge. But eventually, her sincere, scientific way of writing and speaking began to win us all over. I say all, though of course, there were always those who disagreed. But as with most things, public opinion won in the end. And it only takes one clear voice to make a reality out of something that a hundred years before would have been inconceivable. Her arguments were flawless and concise. She found a lawyer to work with her, a policymaker, a correctional officer who had no affiliation with her brother (that way nothing would seem self-interested). I have met Dr. Fortright, and I can tell you, without reservation, that she is one of the most genuine people I know. Her goal was to save lives. Those worthy, or at least more worthy, of saving.

I hope you don't mind if I take a small breather here and tell you about my Sadie. Just as most little girls are to their daddies, Sadie was the apple of my eye. She was the most innocent and mischievous thing you ever laid your eyes on. Her mother, Margot, and I were in our forties when Margot got pregnant. We had been told we couldn't have any more kids. Our only son, Rupert, was twenty-two. He had been a difficult child and grew into an unruly and ferocious man. Of course, we loved him. We were human. However, for our own mental health, we had long ago distanced ourselves from him. We had almost come to terms with the idea that our lives would just be lived between the two of us. So, Sadie was the most incredible surprise. Margot's pregnancy, despite her age, was not difficult. Not as easy as it had been in her early twenties, but she did not complain. In fact, she often tenderly touched her round belly and spoke of how much she loved being pregnant. So, Sadie arrived, and we both instantly knew, in the way only parents can, that this time would be different. She looked at us with such complete trust, such complete and perfect love. Her small dimpled cheeks, her round, soft fists, her smooth, tiny, pink nails. You have truly never seen a more perfect thing in all the world. And this never changed. Where Rupert had begun life pinching, kicking, crying, and sucking on his mother's nipples until they bled, Sadie was gentle, her laughter like a song. Oh, she was still a kid, to be sure, with the silly mischievous ways of kids. She loved licking her fingers and sticking them in the sugar bowl, was always digging for things in her mother's garden and bringing the wriggly, many-legged creatures she found inside to keep as pets, often wanted more than we could give her, and sometimes cried about it.

Sadie was nine when Rupert moved back. She had never met him, and Margot and I rarely spoke of him. We had a few baby pictures in an album, ones where he looked remarkably like Sadie, dimpled cheeks, soft brown curls and all. I never looked at these pictures. They hurt too much. Occasionally Margot and Sadie would. I suppose no matter what your children have done, they are still your children. We found out, much later, that Rupert's movements had been under observation by the FBI for several years. Of course, we didn't know that at the time. How could we have? And though I have often wondered why they didn't do anything sooner, I find that particular thought trajectory is a rabbit hole I'd rather not go down. Besides, I have led a long and happy life and, at my age, I'd rather count my blessings.

Most of you already know some of the story, or at least think you know it. I believe it's now a regular part of high school history curricula. Rupert forced his way back into our lives the same way he forced his way into the world: tearing, screaming, fighting for all he was worth. It was a typical hot midwestern June evening. The air was muggy and the mosquitoes were out in force. I was on the porch with a Miller Light and Sadie was next to me on the swing reading some little novel, something about a spider, a daddy longlegs, I think. Anyway, this black Oldsmobile skidded into the gravel driveway and out of it came a man I didn't recognize. He had thick black hair, almost to his shoulders. He was tanned and muscled and wore tight-fitting dark jeans and a white tank. I kid you not. I didn't recognize him even when he came up the front steps in three long strides and grabbed me by the shoulders, calling me 'Pops'. It wasn't until I got a good look in his eyes, gray and flecked with yellow, like a cat, that awareness came to me.

"And who's this pretty little nugget?" he said, gesturing at Sadie. I didn't want to tell him, but didn't see any way of avoiding it either.

"Well, Rupert, that's your baby sister, Sadie. Sadie, say 'Hi 'to your brother."

I think I must have been in shock, because I don't remember much of the conversation. Mainly I remember Sadie. She was perfectly composed, perfectly polite, perfectly aware of everything that was happening.

"Hello," she said as she stood up and stretched out her small, freckled hand. Her voice was firm and clear, I remember that well, because my own was shaking. For a moment Rupert seemed taken aback by her directness. He paused, turned slightly, and I thought foolishly that he might go. But not Rupert, he was never one to give up. Certainly not when he had set his mind to something.

"Well, hello there yourself," he grabbed her hand and yanked her, hard, towards him, wrapping his huge arms around her, pressing her into him. I was horrified. It made me think of a lion caressing a mouse before he devours it, bones, hair and all.

At first he kept the anger at bay, trying to show us he had changed, but we knew it was just a matter of time. Like a kettle on a fire, at some point it's bound to start boiling. The first time he backhanded Margot across the face, I tried to force him to leave, but he was a very big man with hands the size and strength of two iron pans. I would have called the police, but Margot insisted I didn't. She always felt he was her fault. I wanted to disagree, to comfort her, but the mutation, XYY karyotype, in an ironic twist of fate, is in fact inherited from the mother.

He did not try to hide his jealousy of Sadie. He would go into long, angry tirades and I remember his exact words: "You had the bitch just to spite me, to make sure

I'd get nothing. You never did love me. But you damn sure do love her. The little whore." Margot would lock herself and Sadie in our room and turn the TV or the radio up to drown out the noise. I tried to stay calm, to let him rant, to try my best to understand him and have compassion for him. But mostly, and I'm no longer ashamed to admit it, I hated him. I couldn't stand listening to anyone let into Sadie like that, and I was working on a plan to get him to leave, in the gentlest way possible. I knew we just couldn't go on like this. I'm sure you're wondering about Sadie. She stayed composed through all of it. We explained to her about her brother, about how he couldn't control himself and how ninety-percent of men like him ended up in jail, and how he was just trying to keep his demons at bay. We promised her we were going to do something about it soon. She assured us she was fine. It was during one of these conversations that the part of the story you probably know happened.

He had just wound down from a rage, one where he threatened to kill Margot and I in our sleep and then do away with 'the little bitch', sending us all to where we belonged: hell. He now sat exhausted in my blue armchair, and I thought he had fallen asleep. I went to the room with the girls, trying to comfort Sadie, who for the first time, seemed visibly upset. I was talking quietly, I thought, sharing with her my plan for Rupert's 'relocation 'as I was calling it, hoping to calm her. It turned out, of course, that Rupert was not asleep. He was listening outside the door and when I was through explaining the details, came smashing through it with all the force of his six-foot-four bulldozer body. I was just on the other side of the door but somehow I was thrown in such a way that it only landed on my leg, crushing it just below the knee. I looked down and saw that where it disappeared under the door it lay perpendicular to the knee cap. In the same moment that I realized this, I also realized that Rupert had grabbed his mother by her hair and chucked her, like a doll, across the bed, where she landed with a thunk on the floor between the bed and the dresser, her head smashing into the corner of the dresser just before she landed. I know that after this everything happened quickly, too quickly for either of us to act. I know this because it's what I've been told by forensic scientists, what I've had explained to me, and what, despite my own memory, I've come to accept as true. But in my mind, everything was excruciatingly slow. It was a motion picture run in reverse. Because I knew what Rupert was going to do. He had a knife in his hand, the prettiest little knife I'd ever seen. Silver and shiny, with a smooth black handle. It looked like a toy in his big hands, and part of me thought maybe that's all it was. Sadie began screaming before he reached her. But when he held her down and brought the knife close to her, staring down into her soft blue eyes, she stopped for a moment. I knew what she was thinking: she was thinking he wouldn't do it. Those eyes of hers had won her love her whole life, they wouldn't fail her now. But she didn't know Rupert. He cut them out one at a time while Margot and I watched. While we all screamed.

It was sometime during the trial that Dr. Fortright approached us. She was kind, and tears glimmered at the corners of her eyes when she spoke of our Sadie. We knew she could be trusted; she had been through tragedy too. She was not pushy but laid out, laboriously, the details of law that she and a handful of others had been working on pushing through the legislature. She thought our case could be the clincher, the one to change everything. But, of course, it was up to us. Margot and I talked about it long into the night, long into the foggy hours of the not-quite morning. We talked for days. We laid out each detail, went through them with a fine-toothed comb. Only the most hardened criminals, ones slated for death row or life in prison would be candidates. Each inmate would have a choice. Their parts could be harvested gradually, while they continued to live in the prison, or they could undergo a swift death, whereupon the various organs would be harvested after death. The organs would only go to the most deserving. This meant mainly to children. The belief was that the practice, though perhaps shocking at first, would cut down on incarceration while at the same time saving the lives of many innocents. It would most certainly be embraced by the public, who already felt their taxes were being needlessly wasted on the overwrought prison system. Dr. Fortright and her team had only been waiting for the right moment. They had been waiting for us.

Margot and I talked, but really, we didn't need to. Each time we looked at our Sadie, we knew our answer.

It was a crisp day, mid-November. The leaves were sunset-orange and daisy-yellow outside our window. The doctors had built a make-shift hospital in our home. We had been adamant that there should be no press for this. The home-hospital was their solution. Dr. Fortright took it on herself to guard our privacy. Even making sure the surgeon, anesthesiologist and nurses wore plain clothes, only changing in the bedroom after they arrived. We weren't allowed in the room for the procedure so we sat, rocking restlessly on that same porch that Rupert had taken three long strides to reach just five months before.

Margot squeezed my hand and smiled at me when the surgeon came to get us. "You can see her now," he said.

"She did beautifully, I think you will be very pleased."

He led us to the room, our room, which was now Sadie's hospital room. White and stark and smelling of alcohol. Margot and I each stood on one side of her and took a small hand as they slowly unwrapped the gauze, lifting her head a little where it was tucked underneath. "It's truly astonishing how far we've come with these sorts of surgeries in the last few decades," the surgeon said, smiling. "The recovery time is almost nothing. She'll be able to see you both almost immediately." Her eyelids, under the gauze were pale and ribbed with blue and red veins.

"We're here, darling," her mother said softly. "It's okay now, everything is okay, you can open them."

Slowly, as if small weights held them down, her eyes fluttered open. They looked straight at me, light grey, flecked with yellow, like a cat's.

6. THE LAST TWO WOMEN

From the diary of Rebekah Mechst

May the 30th, Year 2553

Lora and I met when we were children. I can't remember the day although I know there must have been a singular moment in time when our two lives collided. It just seems to me, when I look back on my life, that she was always there. Perhaps we were both at a swimming hole, dressed in slick purple water skins, she with her mother, me with my father. The swimming hole near my home with the deep velvet-blue water, cold as bone, where we often went to play and shared so many secrets. Where she first told me about Greg. Or perhaps it was behind the ruins. Maybe I was sitting cross-legged on the moss-covered ledge under the limestone statue, the one that looks like a man, but with a child's face, the masculine parts removed and replaced with the awkward plaster casting of a lily. Maybe I was reading a book of poems, or maybe writing one of my own, something about a girl drifting aimlessly in a boat to a forgotten island where there still dwelt extinct species of manatee and opossum. Lora was playing hide-and-seek with one of the neighborhood boys, when she bumped into me, and was shocked when she turned around to see the suntanned face of a girl her age smiling, bewildered, up at her. I don't know.

When I think of our childhood I see a still life of the two of us. My father, who had paid a great deal of money to adopt me when I was a baby, not wanting the doctors to change me, believing that we should return to the old ways, had a traveling artist make it. In it we are about seven. It still sits, an icon, on his wide oak desk. Two girls, holding hands, one with a wild crop of short, dark curls, unsmiling, holding a stuffed rabbit, the other blonde and fair and dimpled, nearly a head taller, with a huge carefree smile. I always thought it was the perfect image of us, that somehow the artist must have known our characters in order to capture them with such precision. Later, much later, I came to understand that this view, my view, of both Lora, and our friendship, could not have been more wrong.

June the 1st, 2553

On that blistering June morning Lora still looked like herself. She had always been beautiful. Effortlessly beautiful. Which is the worst kind. Her long honey-blonde hair was pulled up in a ponytail, her large bronze-flecked eyes were rimmed with red, but somehow, not even that detracted from her overall prettiness. Her mother (that word still sticks in my throat, since I never had cause to use it myself), was also beautiful. She was from a long line of Orthodox Jews who emigrated here more than a century ago. Most did not have children, the birthing too painful and the public attention too difficult. But Lora's mother was rebellious and at seventeen gave birth to a healthy baby girl. I, on the other hand, was a genetic engineering malfunction, and never had a mother. Beautiful and with a mother, life certainly wasn't fair. I won't deny that I was jealous of Lora, but I never hated her. I couldn't. I had no one else. It feels silly to me now that it took almost the full twenty-minute ride to figure out what was different about her. You must understand that I was, at that point in my life, living very much within my own mind. But something like a small, blonde mustache on a beautiful woman should have been pretty obvious. Now, so many years later, I can almost laugh about it.

June the 2, 2553

People have always, from the time they reached understanding, striven to look and act like one another. If you peruse old photographs of middle-school students from the early 21st century, you will see what I mean. The male version: think the quintessential pop-stars of that time period. Hair shaven on the sides, long and tousled in front, clothing brandishing the name of whatever store was currently popular, a wounded mysterious expression on every face. The female version: something between blonde bombshell and boho don't-give-a-shit. Anyway, my point is, people have always found a type of person that they think is closest to perfection and tried to imitate it. For a long time that meant two idealized versions, one male, one female. There was an algorithm you could use to see just how perfectly proportioned a person's features were, and then you could get your doctor to essentially give you that face. In the beginning there were always subtle differences, which depended both on the amount of money you could pay for the procedure and the quality of the doctor (though I suppose these are not mutually exclusive).

It was sometime in the early 23rd century that Dr. Gilbert Wong began the experiments that would truly change everything. His daughter, Elizabeth, was born with a vestigial penis (yes, think the high school required reading, *Middlesex*). He and his wife already had two boys and desperately wanted a daughter. But Dr. Wong did not want her to undergo any grueling anatomical surgery. After all, she was his own flesh and blood. He began experimenting in marmosets, tiny tan monkeys with gigantic round eyes and hands like tree-frogs.

At first, he attempted to develop a sort of hermaphroditic XXY monkey. Or maybe that's the wrong word. A neutral monkey. Yes, that's better. Physical neutrality. It didn't work. There was always something inherently male or female about these animals. Some sequence of genetic material that, no matter how he manipulated it, would make the animal just slightly more one way or the other. An aggressive way of approaching other animals versus a desire to nurture, for instance. He began to feel, in some ways, that his experiments were actually confirming stereotypes rather than diminishing them. So his neutralization effort was scratched in favor of a single sex idea. It was easier, he found, to turn a female monkey into a male than the other way around. And he thought, that if he could do one it might open doors to accomplishing the other. So, he began experimenting more with the idea of a single gender. Many of his first experiments were still phenotypically female, XO, without ovaries. A little testosterone at puberty, though, and they looked and acted like males. It was nearly impossible to tell them apart from those born naturally. Dr. Wong still felt that that wasn't enough. They needed to be "fully" male. So the X portion became just a snippet of an X.

I'm not sure if Dr. Wong had any idea what his experiments would eventually lead to. It's an ironic twist of fate that his desire for a daughter created a world with none. He died before he could begin work on creating females, and his daughter and wife both vanished.

Over the course of the next two centuries, physicians and scientists continued Dr. Wong's work, expanding it to human trials. From this was born the idea of a single sex society.

Women, or, at least, feminine women, had become increasingly uncommon. The new "perfect human" had become, possibly as a result of the neutralization efforts, masculinized. It made sense. Women, throughout history, have been oppressed. To be sure, there were great strides made. But, women were always less, and knew it. They were tired of it. They saw a chance to finally, truly, be equal.

Again, the transformations were gradual. If you look back through old magazine files, as I have, you'll see the evolution. Three women sit on a bench, drenched in luminous sunlight. They have lovely, delicate features. Thin, aristocratic noses, large almond-shaped eyes. Two have pencil-thin mustaches, and one a fuzzy tuft of goatee. All three have shaved heads, which, for a while was preferred to the short military cuts that later replaced them. They are dressed in spacesuit green, gray, and dusty blue jumpers. Later, only by studying the photos very carefully, can you distinguish any difference between those who are phenotypically male and those who are not. Perhaps one is slightly shorter, with a more delicate bone structure. Another has spotty clumps of facial hair. But, of course, these things could also be true of even a genuine male. For a long time society existed in this limbo state since the surgery was still too difficult, and a lot of women just weren't willing or didn't have the income to go "all the way".

The problem of children had been solved long ago. Test tube and incubator babies were the norm. More than the norm, they were the only thing. People born "the old way" were freaks and outcasts before they took their first breath. No eggs, no sperm, no in vitro fertilization involved, just simple old-fashioned cloning. Malfunctions like me, like Greg, are either a result of a doctor's mistake or just a random anomaly. A piece of DNA that should produce, say, a person with an IQ of a perfectly acceptable average 110, transforms, and the child has a genius level IQ of 187. Or, in my case, an X(snippet)O that should guarantee a male baby, transforms inexplicably into an XXO. A female. An evolutionary anomaly aimed at preservation, not of the species, but of the irregular.

Many leaders, aided by science, saw the promise in gender and racial neutralization. Most of mankind's strife had sprung from problems with one of the two. If all people were identical, at least on the outside, well, we'd no longer be judging the book by its cover. We'd level the playing field. Like so many things, it started as a desire for peace, for equality. The only thing that had been holding us back was the technology, but with the breakthroughs that continued through the 24th century, that was no longer an obstacle. It is amazing what society can accomplish when nations are in competition to be the first to succeed at something. Nothing like it had been seen since the race for the moon. Suddenly, there were breakthroughs being made everywhere, and a tiny lavender pill was developed in Japan. No grueling series of surgeries, no manipulation of phenotype, no life-long visits to therapists. Even if you were born a malfunction, you could still be normal. To hell with what God had given you.

"What's going on?" Lora said, not looking at me.

"I should be asking you that."

"Oh, this," She stroked the feathery mustache but still wouldn't look at me.

"Yeah, that, want to tell me about it?"

"I just can't do it anymore, Beka. I can't be this symbol you all want me to be. You have to know it's never really been what I wanted. I'm tired of everything being so hard. Why does it have to be so fucking hard? I just want to belong." She was crying. Large tears streaming down her face, distorting her mouth into a thin line, her eyes to slits. Her hair had fallen over one eye and her cheeks were flushed petal-pink. (How could someone cry like that and still look pretty?)" I don't want everything to be so hard. Either people look at me because I'm a girl or they don't because I'm a girl. I'm a walking freak show. Can you understand that? Can't you just understand?"

I suppose I should have felt sympathy, but I didn't. Lora had always been dramatic and usually it just irritated me. Despite the confusion of emotion that was coursing through my hot blood, I could still feel this familiar annoyance beneath. Somehow, it was comforting. Even as I thought, *I should have seen this coming*, I also thought *everything will be okay*. Because we were revisiting our usual scenario where Lora cried about something, and I was annoyed but nonetheless provided a listening ear. Except this time, it was more, and underneath I was terrified.

It's funny, the things that come to mind in a moment of panic. In that car, on that day, I thought of the silliest things. Of the two of us, I was the bigger tomboy. She had always loved the dresses and hair bows her mother made (certainly no-one sold that stuff anymore). She loved being a mom. She breast-fed Stephen until he was two. They did a piece about it in the 'Daily', and she became a sort-of celebrity (she would have called it a 'freakshow item'). She even slept in the bed with him for the entire month he was quarantined for SP107. An act of heroism that was attributed to her femininity, and got us both a lot of positive publicity. I thought we were going to change things, together. Maybe not completely, but at least get them started down a different track. She could show everyone better than I could. She could help them see women didn't have to become extinct, that we could benefit society. That we were necessary. She was married, had a biological son. Maybe one day she could even have a daughter. I had, I realized, put all my hope in her. I tried to slow my breathing. I didn't want to lash out at her.

"What about Greg?"

"He's okay, he'll *be* okay. It hasn't been easy on him either, you know?"

"And Stephen?" I said quietly. Stephen, her son, could not be okay. He loved, no, he adored, his mother. I had been there when she gave birth to him. A soft, round, rosy child who we all wept over. He was six now, and even though I had not been the one to carry him in my womb and deliver him in blood and fury, I loved him as much as any person has ever loved another.

"It will be better for all of us, in the end."

"You can't seriously believe that? After everything you did to fight for this? For what you have? Why would you do this now?" I felt myself, despite the breathing exercise, growing wretched with anger, my voice rising, my heart thumping loud in my chest.

"Greg asked me to."

I could barely hear her when she said this and I had to ask her to repeat it.

"He knows how miserable I've been these last few years. All the publicity, all the hate-mongering. It's just not for me. He loves me, he does. And I was thinking about it too. It wasn't just him."

"Why didn't you tell me this sooner? What will you do? Will you still live together?" The questions poured out of me, a torrent covering my fear. I felt my own hot tears coming and I pressed my fists against my eyelids, trying to stifle them.

"I'm sorry I didn't talk to you before. I know what a shock this must be, but you haven't really been around much lately." Lora looked at me sideways and I turned away from her. "And yeah, I think we'll stay together. He's going to help me get used to everything. We'll help each other, and Stephen of course."

"But..." and I found I didn't quite have the words for a moment. Greg was a man. Not the kind they had been creating for the past two centuries. He was a malfunction, like me. He had sexual drive, something that had essentially been eradicated. He was crazy about Lora. I had my own confused feelings for him, feelings that were unavoidable. How could he possibly be okay with this?

"Beka, He's already made the change." Again, Lora's voice was so quiet I had to ask her to repeat what she'd said. I wished I hadn't. I did not want to hear those words. *Already made the change*. I slid my index finger along the car's security strip and got out. I needed to walk. Lora, thank God, didn't come after me.

We had pulled off into one of the little aerial parks that dotted the cloudless summer sky as far as you could see in either direction. It was the usual 20x20 green square, with intermittent clumps of yellow and white daisies. An iron bench made to look like wood. A round, decorative fountain, filled with blue-gray rainwater. Each park was connected by an aerial path that crisscrossed over the line of lime-white highway. When they were first invented there were several mishaps with them, but eventually, most of the kinks were worked out. Just like with people, I thought. Most of the kinks have been worked out. Except for a few. Lora, Greg, and me. We had been three of those kinks. Now, it was just me. Unless I could somehow change Lora's mind.

If it just wasn't so easy, I thought, breathing in the hot, perfumed air. I had walked across three of the little parks and this one, instead of daisies, was planted with clumps of lilac. Their tiny, star-shaped petals were wilted from the sun, but their smell was still intoxicating. Once upon a time, the change had involved multiple, grueling surgeries, classes to cope with sexual dreams, therapy appointments, etc. Now, most people were just born male, but without the messy stuff like sexual desire or anger management issues. And if, like me, they were an anomaly, a malfunction that was allowed to grow into adulthood (usually because the parents were religious), and decided to undergo the change later in life, well, then there was the pill. A nifty little thing no bigger than a thumbnail that could be taken over the course of a week. No surgeries, no therapy appointments necessary. At least, not usually.

It was far too hot, and I realized, suddenly, that I needed water. My mouth felt as if I had swallowed cotton. I looked longingly at the still, greenish rain-water in the ever-present fountain. That was surely a recipe for some sort of stomach-emptying virus. Instead, I sat on the bench which was shaded at one end by a small potted palm. Someone had taken a great deal of care with this park. Usually there weren't trees.

I tried to close my eyes, but it was too hot, and all I could see every time I did was Greg's face. So different from other men, so alive, so animal. Most men were not large, 5 foot 5. They always sported beards or mustaches, but they were usually of the wispy, barely-there kind. Perfectly coiffed, clean, tidy, gentlemanly. They were fine. They were not Greg. He was rough, he was loud, he had an appetite like a bull. He was, I was sure, very good with his hands. How could Greg have decided to do this? It was, quite simply, impossible.

Lora was lying.

The walk had done its trick. It had cleared my head enough of the initial shock to help me think clearly. There was no way Greg would decide to change. Suddenly, I was desperate to see him. To confirm with my own eyes, that he was still *himself*. I also, simultaneously, felt nauseated at the thought. What if I was wrong? What if, now, where there had been the broad, jovial, intense, living face of Greg, there would be that placid, smiling blankness. I didn't think I could bear it. But why? Why would Lora lie?

She had found out. That must be it.

I will tell you. Greg kissed me. Or I kissed him. Only once, nine months ago. I wanted to know what it was like. Kissing a man who was a man. He had Lora, of course, so it meant nothing to him. He did it, I was sure, just to be nice. But part of me wanted to think it meant more. That he had wondered too, what kissing me would be like. And that is why he did it, not out of pity or kindness, but out of desire. We never talked about it but sometimes there were glances, or hands brushing, or knees touching. I tried my best to forget about it, but it was impossible. I found myself, more often than I care to admit, daydreaming about what it would be like to be in Lora's place. To be his wife, to be Stephen's mother. To have a family of my own. It was a physical ache.

I'll tell you about the kiss. It was, at least for me, an explosion. His lips were warm and sure. He was not timid. His tongue was in my mouth and it searched for mine. It was strange and remarkable to be that close to someone. I think, right at that moment, if he had said he could read my thoughts, I would have believed him. I would have believed anything. My breath stops, caught in my chest like a trapped bird, whenever I think about that day. When I am close to him, it is like it's happening again. That's why I no longer go to their house. I come up with excuses. The usual things: *I'm sick; I have a lot of work to do; I'm tired*. Maybe Lora noticed and asked him. But wouldn't he just have told her he loved her, that it meant nothing? He would have known what to say to put her mind at ease. They could have decided to cut me out of their lives. Why this? Lora, obviously, was really undergoing the change. Unless that was also an elaborate ruse. But that would be too much, even for her. I felt as if my mind was going foggy again. I wasn't thinking clearly. I stood up, intending to continue my walk when a skycycle skidded to a halt next to me, and Greg jumped off.

June the 6, 2553

"Beka, my God, she told me what she said to you." I began to cry, and then to laugh. It was him. It was still him. "I'm so sorry." He grabbed me and pulled me close, wrapping his arms around me. He smelled of earth, warm and heavy and alive. My heart was pounding. I felt flushed and sweaty. I wanted to look at him but was afraid. Gently, he stepped back and lifted my chin with his hand. "Open your eyes," he said. I did. He kissed me then. And it was the same as before. Strong, sweet. But without fear this time. And this time I also knew, he wanted it. After a bit, we sat together on the bench, our fingers entwined. We were quiet for a long time. I didn't want to move, hardly to breathe, for fear somehow I was in a mirage. "You know, she has been talking about this for a long time." It wasn't a question, and he spoke almost in a whisper. "She just didn't want to do it anymore. She said she never really wanted to. She wanted to change since she was a kid. She always wanted to belong. She said you were the only reason she didn't do it before. And Stephen. Not me though. She never said it was me. She wants us all to change. Stephen too, so we can be a normal family."

"Stephen too?" I said, surprised, but also not really. It seemed reasonable if what she really wanted was for them all to be normal. "What did you tell her?"

"I was really angry, at first. Then hurt. Then I tried to listen. The mourning stages, you know?" He looked sad, but somehow, not heartbroken. I looked at him. He hadn't answered my question. My heart started to pound furiously again. Was he saying goodbye?

"It's okay," he said, and I noticed where my nails were digging into his hand, there was blood. He turned it over, stroking the palm with his fingers, smiling. "I told her no. And I told her about us."

"Oh," I said, unable to say anything else. Hoping he would go on.

"She cried and said she already knew. Not necessarily about the kiss. But," he paused and looked at me, almost shyly. "She said she knew that you loved me."

I sucked in my breath. A slow gasp. "Yes," I said quietly, "I think—I think I always have."

"Beka," he said, for the second time, tilting my chin so I had to look at him. "Yesterday, she told me everything. She wanted us all to change because she knew about you. She didn't want you to have us. Stephen and me. The only reason it took her all these years to do it was because she didn't want you to have us." Small, burning tears were squeezing themselves from the corners of my eyes. "I love you too Beka," he said. "I told her I wanted her to be happy, but that I couldn't, I wouldn't do it and I wouldn't do it to Stephen either. I came here to tell you that." He looked at me. I rested my head against his chest. I could hear his heartbeat. A strong, steady beat. A drum-beat. It seemed that my own heart slowed so they were in time with each other. *And the two shall become one*. I remembered the words her mother had spoken at Lora's wedding. We had all the future before us. All the future of the world. I imagined in that moment our entire lives stretched before us. Stephen, our son, grown. Married, perhaps, to one of the girls rumored to still be living in Eastern Europe, where legend had it that Wong's wife and daughter began a monastery for women, though no one has ever found it. Married, and with a son and a daughter of his own. And then, we, my granddaughter and I, would be the last two women.

Suddenly, the strip in my left arm vibrated. I glanced down and saw the small icon with Lora's face appear. I turned it away from Greg, not wanting him to ask about her. Not wanting to break the spell. Three words appeared, in Lora's small, tidy print.

"I love you."

I stood slowly, turning away from Greg, and continued my walk. I did not look back even as he called my name again and again. Not until the sound of it merged with the soft hum of vehicles and insects. By then, he was no more than a black mirage in an unspeakably blue sky.

7. CHILDREN'S RULE

Campbell was trim for twenty-three. He observed himself in the mirror as he always did, studying his face for signs of the first wrinkles, the first gray hairs, waiting for the luster to leave his skin, the shine to be gone from his eyes. He carefully flexed his muscles, feeling for sagging flesh, he smiled and examined his teeth, looking for spots of brown, for receding gums. That morning, he found it. A single white hair among the black. It was in his beard. He plucked it carefully with the nail of thumb and index finger, and wept.

Each child, of course, is still a treasure, still a miracle. And yet sometimes the miracle is muted by the fear. They never speak of it, Campbell thinks. He and Francine certainly never do, but as far as he knew, neither did anyone else. If anyone dared to speak such things aloud, it would be Mary, with her obnoxious inability to filter anything. She'd been embarrassing him since they were children. When he was seven and she four, "Why do your ears stick out like that?", "What're those spots all over your arms?" and once "Why does your thing look like a sausage?" She asked these questions, with big, innocent eyes. He could almost believe in her naivete, but he knew her too well for that, knew how her mind worked, knew she was goading him. When he was eleven, and Francine was first brought to their house, Mary said, in a voice she pretended was a whisper (but everyone could hear)" look at the jugs on her. She'll make enough milk to feed an army." Campbell blushed with shame, but Francine only looked away, pretending not to hear. Of course, then, none of them had been named Campbell, or Francine, or Mary. They were lucky. He had friends with names like Smurfette or Iron Man. He'd heard of Venom or Dick being names too, but most children, by the time they did the naming, were mature enough to at least choose something nice, something heroic, or nostalgic. The parents were careful to cultivate these emotions. They knew it would benefit them later.

Mary had never followed any of the rules. And she had paid for it dearly. He should not feel sympathy for her. She was always too headstrong; she should have seen it coming. The name should have warned her. Mary. Not the "quite contrary "one, she might have liked that, nor the "Magdalene," which also might have pleased her, but the other one, the "mother of God" one. The virgin queen of heaven. That was like a slap in the face. She never tried to hide the grimace each time they called it. "Mary, Mary, Mary," he sometimes yelled, or sang, depending on his mood. Payment for all the times she goaded and embarrassed him. After, though, he wished, no, longed, to have been there for her. A brother she could confide in, a brother she could turn to, a brother who would protect her. *Protect her from what?* He though, defensively. *From her own children?* she should have been kinder to them, especially the boy. She should have seen that her incessant teasing only angered him. The way she pushed boundaries, made him wary of her, which made him dangerous. She was never cut out for motherhood. Perhaps, in the end, it was a mercy her son had given her.

Then, though, they were still just called by the things that seemed to define them best. Campbell was known as Peach, for the way his cheeks turned a pastel shade of pinky-orange whenever he was embarrassed, which, with Mary as his sister, was often. Francine had been introduced to them as Sweetie. Sometimes parents did that, trying to project their desires on their child. Often, it backfired. In Francine's case, it was perfectly, dully, accurate. Mary was Vex, short for vexing. Campbell had come across the word in a book, and used it on her one day when she was being terrible. It stuck. Sometimes names changed as children grew, but often, the first impression was the one that stayed. Now, though, he was Campbell, he had always been Campbell. Campbell would be on his tombstone, the only name anyone would ever remember. The name his daughter had given him. Her favorite soup. He liked to think it brought fond memories for her. But he neither sought for nor expected an explanation.

They had called her Joy, before, in the time he wasn't supposed to think about. Now she was mother, and he was child. She named him, and their lives had been reborn. He should not think of her as Joy, especially now that he had begun the deterioration process. He might be able to hide it for a few months still. But soon, when the skin around his neck became loose, when the flesh under his eyes formed gray pockets, when his hands became bones and sinew and the wrinkles at the corners of his eyes and mouth appeared, there would be no hiding it. He might have a year left, two if he was very lucky. Anything more than that would be a false hope. A lie that he could not afford to treasure. And yet, who among them did not treasure it? Who among them did not hope? Who among them did not lie?

"Campbell," called a small, shrill voice, "Campbell, Campbell, Campbell," with increasing urgency. Campbell dropped the hair in the toilet and flushed. "Here, I'm right here." His voice was clear, not a hint of fear. Not a drop of uncertainty. Nothing to make her suspicious, and yet, she hesitated in the doorway, looking at him steadily with clear, gray, unblinking eyes. Of the two children, she had taken to her role most naturally. This had surprised Campbell. He thought it would be hardest for her.

She had been such a wonderful child. A delight, a pure joy, others might have said in a time long ago. When she was born, and he watched Francine, who was still Sweetie, suckling her, he had been overwhelmed with feeling. This must be what love felt like, he thought. She was curious, affectionate, even compassionate. Rescuing earthworms from the pavement after the rain. Life and joy seemed entirely inseparable in her small body. Now, looking at her, the vague fear, the clenching and unclenching in his chest, it was difficult to reconcile her as that same child. The confusion of feelings broke his heart, and he wondered, for a moment, if she felt the same way. If he suddenly enveloped her in his arms, would she sob against his shoulder, relief flooding through her? He pictured it. He would never know the answer to that question.

The naming took place on a Monday. The children's independence had taken place on a Monday as well. That was a Monday long before Campbell, or any of them, had been born. A time when the world was in chaos. When the aging virus changed the first person, and then fifty, and then five hundred, until finally the entire population was infected. Children roamed the streets aimlessly. And their parents, frail, ancient, devoid of all cognitive faculty, still attempted to run things. That was a time of terror.

When Joy walked down the stairs, she already looked different. More angular. That's what he had thought, even though she couldn't possibly have changed. Not from one day to the next. She had been very young for marriage, only nine. He wondered if she would be ready. Marriage was one thing. This shifting of roles was something else entirely. It appeared he need not have worried.

He barely remembered his own ceremony. The one where he named his mother. The boy for the mother, the girl for the father. One of each. A perfect little family. The boy, after the marriage and naming, went to live with his wife's family. It was easier that way. Everyone had their place. He had named his mother Rose, because he loved her, because she was beautiful. Also, because she had a sharp side, a dangerous side. It's where Mary had gotten it from. Also, he knew she would love the name, and he still wanted to make her happy. Even though he knew, soon, it wouldn't matter. She had been pleased with the name. He could tell by the way her eyes sparkled and danced, even though her face was impassive and unsmiling.

Joy, or Mother now, had taken his hand firmly in her own, and placed it on the slab. Then she had tied the ribbon, half white, half black, around his hand, binding it to the slab. Her fingers were deft. She must have practiced.

Their guard stood to one side, unsmiling, gun thrown over his shoulder. He couldn't have been more than ten, Campbell thought. Young to be a guard. He thought he remembered that they had to be married first. Usually the marriage did not take place until closer to twelve or thirteen. The timeline for childhood was still relatively unchanged, and most did not reach puberty before then. The guard was hardly ever necessary anymore; it was a remnant of an older society, a society that still occasionally rebelled.

She tied the ribbon, and then. And then. His mind always trailed off here. The memory of pain, even after three years, still too sharp, too real.

"Campbell," the voice was a command. He looked up, startled. What had he been doing? Standing there like an idiot. She would know something was wrong. "Are you okay?"

"Yes, Yes, of course, I'm fine."

"Good." She sounded so grown up, he thought, and he felt proud, even as the familiar wariness settled into his bones. "I need you to get Francine. Wit and I need to talk to you. Together." Wit was their boy. Called that for his incorrigible love of jokes. Joy was still permitted to use the name, as were the other children. "What did the brother call the party he invited his sister to?—A BarbieQ," "Why wouldn't the skeleton cross the street?—Because he didn't have any guts," and so on. Of course, Wit no longer told those jokes. At least not in their company. He saved that side of himself, now, as they all did, for the other children. The adults were no longer privy to such things.

"Of course," he said to her, turning to go, keeping his

eyes lowered. He saw that he would have to brush past her to get out. He waited for her to move from the doorway, and when she didn't, he tried to walk by, pressing himself as close to the wall as possible. Still, she didn't move, and he felt her warm skin brush against his like a burn. As soon as he was past, he rushed from the room. She could have him beaten for that, or worse. But she did not follow. She did not sound an alarm.

He found Francine sitting in her room. Her back was to him. She seemed to be looking out the window. A window that opened onto a mulberry tree, ripe with dark purple fruit. She turned and he saw that her lips were stained nearly black with the fruit. She held out a clenched hand to him, and he saw that she had crushed the berries in her fist, so the juice dripped down the inside of her pale arm, like a trickle of blood. He went to her then, and held her, and she sagged against him. Her breath was already shallow and he could see the gray hairs like spider webs spreading out from the edge of her scalp. He knew this was the way it would happen. The way it had been happening for a hundred years. And yet, it was still a shock. "Come," he said, softly, "the children are waiting."

Joy sat, straight and still, on the couch. Her face was unreadable, impassive. Joy's husband and Wit's wife were not there, so this was something just between the four of them, Campbell thought, his wariness rising. Wit sat next to her, close enough that she could reach out and touch him. He was not so impassive. A small smile played at the corner of his mouth. As if he had a joke he was savoring on the tip of his tongue. When they saw Francine, who walked listlessly behind him, he thought he saw a small twitch at the corner of Wit's eye, and that Joy clenched her hands together more tightly. But perhaps he only imagined those things. If they had twitched, or clenched, he would not have blamed them. The deterioration was shocking.

"You can go," the guard looked at her and hesitated, "now." She said, and it was a command. He went.

Campbell felt confusion wash over him. What was she doing? They could all get in trouble for this. Get in trouble, or worse. "Come here, Campbell," she said, "You can bring her too," gesturing with her head at Francine who was twirling one long, grey lock of hair round and round her index finger. She was fading very quickly, Campbell thought, unusually so. Just yesterday, her eyes were still bright. She whispered that she loved him when he passed by her room. She must not have taken her pill; it was the only explanation for having those kinds of feelings. The pills were prescribed at the same time as the naming, so they would live together as brother and sister now (the daughter and her husband were now their parents). Campbell took his each morning, then again, at night, for good measure. He didn't like having the dreams. They made him wake with a vicious longing and hunger, picturing Francine's smooth, fragrant body, her voluptuous round breasts, her oval mouth. It was better not to remember these sorts of things. Maybe Francine, like him, had found the first signs, a few weeks ago, maybe even months ago, and had hidden them. Maybe she knew she didn't have much time left. He could understand wanting one more day. It's what they all wanted. If she had told him, would he have gone to her? Kissed her stomach, sucked on her ripe nipple, entered into her? Would he have done that for her? No, he thought, no, he would not. His own life was too valuable to him.

“I’m sorry,” Joy said, when he was beside her, “I’m sorry about—” for a moment he thought she was about to say Mother, and his heart caught in his throat,“ her,” she finished, closing her eyes for a moment, as if she needed to compose herself. “She told me several months ago. But it has taken her very quickly. I thought she would have more time.”

“Yes,” said Campbell, “yes—” he stopped for a moment, puzzled. “You knew? And you kept her here?”

“Yes,” Joy replied, and suddenly she looked so much older than her twelve years, so tired. “It was my choice to make.” Then again, “I hoped she would have more time.”

Wit began to laugh, not a happy laugh, but a bitter sort of sound, a cackle, like a hyena. Joy and Campbell looked up. Francine was rolling on the floor, like a dog or a horse with an itch. Rolling back and forth, legs and arms in the air, thrashing wildly. Campbell stared at her, unable to move. A madwoman, he thought. Would that happen to him too? Better to head out well before that. Better to leave with a little bit of dignity.

In a moment, she stopped, and lay very still, staring at the pocked ceiling and the fan that circled round and around. Her eyes followed it, making her look almost crazier than when she had been thrashing about. Joy returned her attention to him, and he tried not to look over at Francine. “I called you here, the three of you, to tell you something.” She paused, looking at him and Wit gravely. “I’m going to have a baby.” Wit looked, for an instant, at Campbell, and he thought he saw compassion in Wit’s eyes.

“Congratulations, little sister,” he said, “I’m very happy for you.” Campbell’s heart sunk. So he was out of time, after all. On to the mines or the factories with Francine. There was no longer a place for him here.

Joy reached out and touched the tip of Campbell's arm, the nub where his hand used to be. He almost flinched, but she was very gentle. "I'm sorry," she said.

"Sorry?" she wasn't supposed to be sorry. It wasn't as if it were her fault. She just did what she was supposed to do. She was keeping order in the world. Campbell had been proud of how quickly and unsympathetically she had done it. *With precision and valor. So we all remember our place.* She spoke the words and then took his hand in one swift motion.

"You can stay," she said, almost a whisper. "I was going to tell Francine too. I was going to keep you here as long as possible. I might still even be able to keep her. Whenever they discover her, we can say the change came on too quickly, that we only just knew." So that was why she'd dismissed the guard, Campbell thought. He glanced over again at Francine. Impossible. But him? Perhaps. He felt something soar in his chest, a lightness, a hope. "Wit will help us," she continued, "he doesn't want you all to end up in one of the mines either. Do you know what they're like?" Campbell shook his head. He'd heard some stories, mostly scary bedtime stuff Mary had told him. He didn't know what was actually true and what was her vicious imagination, though. "Wit's been there. It's horrible. You would not see the sun again. You would mine the ore until your body gives out or until you are slowly eaten away by parasites and bats." Wit nodded.

"Yes," he said, "yes, I've seen it."

Campbell felt sick.

He had a sudden vision of his mother. Her pretty, pale, laughing face, being eaten by a little gray bat. The eyes first, he remembered Mary saying. They always go for the eyes first. They crave the liquid. Why had he never tried to find out more himself? It was easier just to believe what you were told, he thought. So much easier.

"Here," Joy held out her hand, "this is for you. I've been waiting a long time to give it to you." It was a small brown box, just the plain cardboard kind things are packed in. He opened the flaps on the side, which weren't sealed. Inside was a single red rose. Only the flower, no stem or leaves attached. It was dried, so it had the color of old blood. Somehow, it was still fragrant, and Campbell found himself inhaling the sweet, slightly sickening perfume.

"Where?" was all he could say. There were no roses, that he knew of, anymore.

"I thought you would like it. I thought it would remind you of grandma."

"Grandma?" the word was strange. An ancient word. An obsolete word. No one here had grandparents.

"I remembered." Joy said, looking steadily at him. Yes. Yes. He did too. He had told her the story, when she was a small child. About his mother's naming. She was so small, only two or three. He only told her because he did not think she would ever remember it. Or maybe he hoped she would remember it? He didn't really know which. Anyway, it took his breath that she did.

"Here, take this." It was Wit this time, and he was holding out a single translucent, oval pill.

"What is it?"

"It will help you remember."

"Help me remember?" Campbell didn't understand, but he took it, swallowing it with a mouthful of saliva.

"You should sit down" Wit said, "This might hurt."

Campbell was about to ask why, when it hit him. Like a gut punch, but one that socked through his entire body. He doubled over, and vomited. Everything came back to him. Everything, and all at once. Joy's birth, and Wit's. His wedding day. Francine's timid, hopeful eyes on his. His parents, Rose and King, leaving their home for good. But it was not the memories that sent him to his knees; he'd always had those. It was the emotion behind them. An emotion other than fear. The only one the other pill seemed to keep intact. Emotion he had felt, but forgotten entirely. Or been incapable of feeling. Tears blinded him, and he began to hiccup violently.

"Oh my God, oh my God." Was all he could say, over and over again.

Joy came then, and put her hand on his shoulder, and kissed the place where his hand had been.

"I know," was all she said, and it was enough.

When he could finally gather himself together enough to sit up, he went to Francine. He held her for a long time. He whispered that he loved her too. She said nothing, but that didn't matter.

"There are still good people in the world." Joy said, "A lot of us. It's because we had parents like you."

"There's a lab, secretly working on a cure. They're getting pretty close," Wit said.

“A cure? But I thought the virus mutated too rapidly for there to ever be a cure?”

“Have humans ever encountered anything that they could not eventually overcome? The problem is, there are a lot of the children that don’t want a cure. You know how things used to be--before. It wasn’t so great for us then.”

“Yes. I suppose I can understand that. So what now? What do I do?”

“We thought you and Fran—and Mom, could stay here and we would figure it out as we go along.”

“I’ve started deteriorating too,” Campbell said. I found the first sign yesterday. “You know we can’t stay. I won’t let you and Joy risk yourselves like that. Especially now that Joy’s expecting.”

“Let us worry about that,” Joy said, glancing at Wit. Campbell paused, for a moment, looking back and forth between them. He felt so much pride, so much love, like his chest would explode with it.

“I love you both,” he said, and then, “GUARD!” with a loud smack of his palm against the door. The boy entered immediately. He must have been waiting just outside the door. “We have to leave. My wife and I are both deteriorating, and my—” He looked at Joy then, and smiled, “my daughter is going to have a baby.” The guard looked stunned, but it was only for an instant, a nearly imperceptible instant. He was evidently well trained. He reached down to jerk Francine to her feet. “Never mind about that. We’ll both come willingly enough.” Campbell reached out and took Francine by the hand, pulling her gently to her feet. “It’s time for us to go now, sweetheart.”

At the door, he glanced back one last time, and saw, with enormous pleasure, that his children sat, hand in hand, tall, straight-backed, unreadable. And all was as it should be.

8. DON'T LOOK TOO CLOSE

Carma and Joseph walked hand in hand down the narrow, slick sidewalk, weaving in and out of the people milling about in the damp twilight. It was a typical Seattle dusk. The air was heavy with moisture, the cold settling under their jackets and beading on Carma's red beanie. Joseph's breath was visible with each exhale. The bars were already filling with tourists, enticed by the salt scent of fish and sweet-sour of beer. Carma and Joseph were locals, and they sped past, headed to a more private haunt, The Unlikely Neighbor, an attempt to re-ignite a passion for British pubs, turned local favorite. Good beer, decent food, blessedly off the beaten path. They passed the knitting shop oddly sandwiched between Sex Toys and Extreme Lingerie. It never failed to make Carma giggle. It's what she loved about this city. They also passed the woman. The same one who almost always sat on this corner, covered in shadows. Same sign. Too personal. Shameless, really. The homeless population was out of control, Carma commented, not for the first time. Joseph nodded his agreement as they hastily side-stepped around her. For some reason, probably because he grew up with a father who couldn't pass someone by without offering to buy them a burger, Joseph glanced behind him and noticed that the woman had fallen forward over her sign so the only visible words were "my life" at one end and "like yours" at the other. She didn't even look alive. He walked more quickly, speeding Carma along with him.

This morning was the same as each of the almost 4800 days before it. The same as almost every day since she gave birth to her first child. The baby was still sleeping at 7:22 when Sara went into her cool, dark room. It smelled of baby things, of soft floral Johnson soap, of a not unpleasant hint of sour milk and fresh laundry. It smelled of *her*. She was curled in her bed, knees bent under her, small round bottom slightly in the air, hands tucked beneath her spaceship pajamas, fists clenched to stay warm. Sara stood by the bed and watched the baby's small back rise and fall, then crouched down to make her face level with the slats so it would be the first thing she saw when she opened her eyes. "Good morning my darling one," she murmured. The baby stirred and turned her head towards Sara's voice. "Good morning my love," she whispered again. The baby opened her eyes and pushed herself to sit, reaching her chubby arms towards Sara, fingers opening and closing, her gesture of wanting. Wanting out and into her mother's arms. Sara lifted her and held her tightly and the baby circled her arms around her mother's neck, legs around her waist, head pressed against her shoulder. Usually Sara made coffee while getting the other two ready for school, and the baby sat on her hip, propped in the crook of her arm, watching, an extension of the mother. Today, Sara had no stomach for coffee. The thought of it turned in her, souring already in her mind. For two days she had barely eaten: a few pretzels, a slice of banana that immediately turned to bile. She thought her milk would dry up, but it didn't. She was hearty. She had lasted this long.

She thought, briefly, of telling Sam. But she knew that, if she did, it would be impossible for her to go through with everything. Besides, Sam would beg to go with her. She just wanted the chance to explain, to say goodbye, at least to him. To tell him she would be waiting for him when he was old enough and ready to find her. To tell him her reasons. All the reasons she had listed again and again to herself. He might understand, in this moment, when he still loved her. He might. He asked her once, when he found her curled up, crying on the bathroom floor, why she stayed. Even then, barely ten, he knew a woman shouldn't stay with a man like that. And he loved his father too. The baby and Eva knew nothing. Eva would remember her mother a little, Sam more; the baby, who every moment of the past year has been devoted to, would have no memories at all. Maybe the other two would tell her stories about Sara; how she sang to them and taught Eva to paint and Sam to sew. Or maybe they would hate her forever and would never speak her name.

She thought at first of going far, to Spain or France or Greece, even Germany, but she quickly realized that would not be necessary. As long as she left the children he would never look for her. And she needed the children to be able to find her, if, when the time came, they wanted to. Her husband would not talk about or think about her and he wouldn't let them either. He was too proud. It would be, for him, as if she never existed. She wondered if he would re-marry. Maybe. It was impossible to know anything about him, she could only guess at what he would do. He would work more but still be a good father. He was always a good father. That was the only way this could work, otherwise she would have stayed, even if it killed her.

She bought soft, comfortable clothing, layers that she could wear from the still-summer heat of Georgia fall to the crisper, drearier weather she was going to. She knew she wouldn't be buying expensive clothes like this anymore. She brought nothing old, nothing with the smell of this house. When she got there, she would cut her hair too. It fell to the middle of her back now, in dark gold cascades, thick and soft. He loved her hair. She would cut it to her chin. Maybe shorter.

The city she decided on was a place of travelers and misfits, where no one would care about her past. She practiced lies though, just in case. *Where are you from?* North Carolina (she had lived there for a while when she was a teenager, and still had an aunt in Charlotte who she could claim as proof). *Where did you go to school?* She would tell them she didn't go. Even though she had a bachelor's in art, she never used it, and it felt most of the time like it never happened. She had already secured a job waitressing at a little bar and it was better in those sorts of jobs not to seem too educated. *Have you ever been married? In love?* No and no. That part of her life she would erase entirely.

The first time it was bruises blooming purple-blue and lurid-red on shoulders and spine. Her memory was not good, but when she closed her eyes, or even, sometimes, when they were open, she could see those moments perfectly. Hunched by the bathroom, arms circling her abdomen, protecting the little thing inside. In the morning he never believed he did it. Even when she tried to show him the evidence, somehow, he could not see. It had only been physical a handful of times, though each though each time was more violent, Sara was able to forget, to live in the times in between, and believe it would not happen again. But it was becoming harder to forget. Two weeks ago it was her body-slammed against the wall, head butting into her face until her lip burst and blossomed red. Her eye swelled shut. She lied to the children and did not leave the house. Of course, he imagined it away. She fell, and he believed the lie. She was beautiful, he said, a week later when the bruises were almost gone. The best mother, the best wife. He loved her so much, he couldn't live without her. Sweet words. But when she saw herself, this cowering, fearful, weeping and hysterical woman, she could only hate him. There was no love left in her.

The boy next to her was dark haired, like Sam. Tall, maybe seventeen. His eyes were dark though, whereas Sam's were two amber cat-eyes. In just a few short years Sam would be this boy and she would not know him. If she saw him on a plane, would she recognize him? The baby, she knew, she would see in every face, forever. Every fair, blonde girl would be her. But Sam, her first, stoic, honest, best boy, how could she ever not know him?

Her heart was solid stone. It had become so heavy that it seemed it would drop out of her and roll across the ground, demolishing all in its way. She did not cry.

At 11:30 she took the baby into the room to nurse her. Sara cradled the baby's soft head and the warm skin of her face against her chest and the baby opened her small pink mouth to her. She let her nurse for nearly an hour, until she was breathing soft and slow and Sara knew she would not wake. She would regret it later, this indulgence. She would swell and harden, engorged with milk and no baby to feed. They would long for each other, mother and child. But as her engorgement subsided, she would know that the child's time of needing her for nourishment was also fleeting.

She would start again, but would have no more children. She made certain of that before she left, with a final appointment to the OB/GYN who had delivered all three of her children. The three were all she wanted. If the children ever looked for her, she needed them to know that no one had replaced them.

At first, she thought she would leave and take the children. This thought was easy, happy. She imagined all the days of sunshine, of laughter, dancing in the kitchen, cookie dough and sewing projects. Days free of fear. She would sue for sole custody. But no matter how hard she tried, or how vivid her ideas, she knew she could not give them anything close to the life they had. Also, he would never let them go.

He was a very good father. Attentive, and encouraging, he did homework with them whenever he was around. Even though he was so busy he found time to take them to all the Star Wars movies and went fishing and swimming, sometimes even camping. Sara's friends, in fact, were jealous. He was amazing, they said. They wished their husbands worked so hard and still made time for them, they said. She knew he would take care of the children. And once, whatever it was in her that drove him to insanity was gone, he could be a good man in reality. Maybe one day God would forgive them both.

“Mama?” a face already growing long, losing its baby softness peered up through long pale lashes and a fuzz of thick curls still fluffed from sleep.

“My gorgeous girl,” Sara pulled her close, kneeling, looking into her mischievous eyes. “You are so beautiful, so smart, so strong.” She wanted to say everything, to record it so Eva could hear it again and again. Anytime she doubted her own perfection, Sara wanted her to hear her mother’s voice. She wanted to tell Eva to never never think she did this because of her. She was everything. It was the hardest and best thing she could do.

“Do you want to stay home and bake today? Skip school?”

“Yes!” Eva’s face brightened at this small, unexpected gift. At least they would have one more perfect day together. Although perhaps she would only remember it as a lie. As the day her mother left without even saying goodbye. Sara pulled out *Baking with Chocolate*“ what do you want to make? Anything, it’s your choice.” Eva flipped through and landed on a beautiful red-velvet cupcake with peaks of white and dark chocolate icing piled in perfect turrets.

“This one, can we make this one?”

“Yes, of course!” Sara tried to sound as joyful as the girl, but suddenly, she was tired. So tired. She didn’t know how she would make it through the rest of this day. She heard his voice echoing through all the words she spoke, making them false. He came home to discover that she had absentmindedly thrown two silk ties in with the regular wash. They were crumpled and puckered, unrecognizable. She shouted that it was all she could do just to care for the kids, that she was tired of feeling like his slave, of living in fear of doing anything wrong. That she had given up everything for him. It always started like this and then spiraled out of control. "Bitch. Whore. Good for nothing whore." His voice was hard, full of loathing. He had said the same or similar words to her countless times before and she had been able to wash them away in the morning, but this time they seemed etched into her hands, they came out with each breath, they circled and landed on the counter and formed into fog on the windowpane.

Sara pretended she was just going on a little trip; she would see the children again. She would enjoy herself for a few days, that's all. But, no, that sort of pretending would not do. She was remaking herself. She was free of him. She was still young and pretty. She had nothing to weigh her down. One small brown carry-on with everything in it. She brought no pictures. That was the hardest choice. She knew she had to stop remembering, that anything else would be debilitating. She opened an account in only her name, transferring $50,000 from their joint account. She had always dealt with all the finances, and her husband didn't even notice. Anne, a lawyer, and one of her few true friends suggested this, assuring her he wouldn't ask about the money. Anne convinced Sara that it was very little, considering everything she did for him and what he would now have to pay someone to take her place. She would need the money to get started, no doubt. Anne had seen these kinds of things unfold a hundred times. Anne was the only person she confided in. Even then, it was only a partial confession. She barely mentioned the verbal abuse, saying nothing of the physical things. In this, too, she was protecting him, protecting them. Anne tried to persuade her to divorce with dual custody, but eventually, after going around and around for weeks, looking at every angle, had given up. Sara was adamant that her husband's name stay intact. For the children. She did not want him to lose his job, or status in the community. The results would be catastrophic. Sam was on a path to the Ivy league, Eva not far behind. She would never take that from them. Their father's reputation for brilliance, innovation and compassion in the medical community was far-reaching. Being a wife-beater, even the rumor of such a thing, could ruin a man and his family. She had witnessed it first hand when a colleague early on in their marriage had gone through such accusations. No one won in those cases. Sacrifice meant giving up yourself for those you loved. That was all she was doing. Nothing more. Nothing less. She didn't tell Anne the secret she kept hidden almost from herself. That she also had to escape from him, break cleanly away, finally have a life of her own.

Sara was in the final boarding group and waited until close to the end to get on. She pulled her small brown bag down the aisle, her backpack strapped across the handle. When she got to her seat there was hardly any room in the overhead. "I think there's some space here," a man said, "let me give you a hand". Sara nodded, grateful for the kindness and glanced at him quickly. He was tall and thin, a bit older than her, she thought. Brown, thick hair and glasses. He looked at her almost shyly and she felt a twinge of embarrassment.

"Thanks," she murmured, looking for her seat number. "Uhm, I think I'm 34F, next to you."

"Oh, pardon me," he moved down a few steps to let her by. Thoughts of what could happen sitting next to this stranger for the next six hours darted through her mind.

She turned away so he wouldn't see the color rise to her cheeks.

They sat close, she by the window, he in the center. There was no one next to him, but he did not move to the empty seat. His arm slipped past the barrier of their separate chairs to brush hers. Neither of them pulled away and this sent a thrill through her. He pretended to look out of the window, but she knew he was studying her. She tried to seem oblivious, pulling out a book of short stories she had purchased in the airport shop. She let her hair fall across her shoulder and a little into her eyes, knowing this made her look prettier. After a moment, he pulled out a book too and pushed the glasses up the bridge of his nose. He had been careful not to move his arm from where it touched hers. She imagined falling asleep and waking to find his hand in hers, or even, his lips on hers. She immediately felt foolish. Was she that desperate to start again, now? It was shameful. Deciding, suddenly, nervously, to make the first move, she rested her small cold hand on his thigh. He did not move. She hazarded a glance and saw the wedding ring which she had not looked for before. Her eyes moved to his face, forming a question. His mouth was slightly open. She had been too preoccupied to notice the soft snoring. She pulled away carefully, re-adjusting her body to look out the window, hunkering down in her corner.

She had to learn to be alone.

Her husband was no fool. He quickly realized what she had done. She had, in fact, ceded all parental rights. It was the only way she could see of being completely free of him. She had given him the chance, too, to start again, while still keeping everything. The divorce was quick and simple, as far as those things go. It surprised her when he let Sam write. Which Sam did, every week, in the beginning. Then, of course, as he grew older and time lessened his sorrow and his need for her, it was less often. But she understood. She was thankful for what she had. He sent her pictures too, of Eva, of the baby who already she barely recognized. They were both so beautiful and it made her ache again for them, but it was a soft, dull thing, nearly bearable. She met men and dated a few. They were attractive and kind, never too intelligent: A bartender, a soccer player. She was careful that nothing got serious. Sometimes there were nightmares, things that made her wake shivering, whimpering. Once she glimpsed a man from behind that had her husband's haircut and shuffling walk. She was sick for three days, barely able to leave her small apartment. Then Sam came to visit. He was eighteen and at first she shied away from him. He was his father, in face and form and voice. Tall and handsome. Only his eyes were different, allowing her to get her bearings. They hugged, and cried, and laughed. She showed him her city and it was as if they had always been together. Those were the best days of her life.

He returned to start school at Emory where he would study chemistry, on his path to medical school. He continued to write. He loved school. He was doing well, as she knew he would. He met a girl, Cynthia. She was pre-med too and her laugh reminded him of Sara. He satiated his need for creativity by teaching himself to knit. He made her a beautiful gold and purple scarf, soft and thick and warm, smelling of cinnamon.

Many of his letters were about Eva. Eva was morose. Eva was not interested in her friends and was doing poorly in school. Their father, who Sam hardly ever mentioned, had found Eva kissing a girl. Sam thought Eva was doing drugs. The picture Sam sent was of a wan girl, pale and delicate, her hair dyed raven's black, small silver bars through eyebrow and nose. Sara tore the picture into tiny pieces and put them down the garbage chute. On her fridge she left the one of the honey-haired, smiling, eight-year-old she knew. Eva used to write too and sometimes there was a small, meticulous water-color tucked inside. In those letters she was still dancing and was teaching the baby to paint. The baby had started kindergarten. She had spilled grape juice on Eva's favorite dress and liked to wear her sister's shoes around the house. Eva did not visit, and Sara did not ask her to. She wanted it to be the girl's choice, and was unsure if her father had already said no. Almost a year before, the letters from her had stopped. She sent a final watercolor. In it a storm lurched across the purple sky and the woman looking up at the clouds had no face. Sam pleaded with Sara to come. He was very alarmed. Eva was worse. He thought she could help. But Sara could not go, he had to understand that. He did not write for several months. Then in December, a week before Christmas, she received a letter from him that she could barely read. It was scrawled in thick black ink, one word joining into the next so she had to study it carefully to understand what it said.

Eva was dead. The baby, now in second grade, found her in their shared room, hanging from the ceiling fan. In the last line, the one she would hear whispered like a private, insidious mantra for the remainder of her life, every blow, every insult coalesced inside of her. Everything she spent the past seven years trying to eradicate rushed back in terrible force. She howled until she was sure someone would come. She retched. Then she curled in the corner, forehead to the ugly grey carpet, repeating his words over and over, singing them, shouting them, murmuring them: "I will never speak to you again. I never want to hear your name or the sound of your voice. It will be as if you never existed. Eva's death is on you."

***

Joseph went back the next day. He was alone this time and it was earlier, less crowded. Most people were just home from work and had not ventured out yet to fill the streets and the bars. Still, he felt conspicuous, maybe more so because of the lack of people. He glanced around swiftly before dropping a few coins in her tin bucket. They made a clanging sound in its empty bottom. She had been hunched over in the same listless manner as before, but the noise alarmed her to life. She looked up at him languidly and he was startled to see a row of small, nearly perfect white teeth smile at him. Her hair was thick and matted and mostly gray but in between he could see the color had once been a deep blond. Her skin was mottled with age spots but otherwise surprisingly free of wrinkles. He glanced around again, nervously, the few people passing by paid him no more mind than they did her. She had a heavy scarf wrapped tightly around her thin neck, purple and gold. She was probably warmer than him, he thought. Adjusting the faux-fur collar on his jean jacket, he bent over the sign which was now visible in its entirety, but noticing suddenly that a young woman across the street was watching him, he didn't read it.

9. I'M STILL HERE

Colleen is dead.

Three days ago.

They had given her one year.

In nearly every significant way we led parallel lives. Both diagnosed at 30, both elementary school teachers with four children and a fifth life growing within us even as death also grows, unknown. So many similarities, and a few nearly imperceptible things, that made all the difference.

I have said her name in my sleep and it courses through my waking hours too, again and again, as if it were my own. I am terrified that she will be forgotten.

Her children will surely always remember. They are her legacy. Yes, but they must grow up, live their lives, in many ways forget in order to heal. Never forget entirely, of course, but enough that her memory is relegated to a small compartment in their minds that can be locked and unlocked at will. Not the continuous aching fresh loss it is now. She would never want them to live with that. And yet she wants to be real to them, forever. At each significant moment in their lives-- marriage, the birth of their own children, all of the milestones we share, she will come flooding back to them. She wants this, even as it will bring its own renewed heartbreak. The PINK concert she took her daughter to, the trip to Disney she somehow managed to bring them on, the hundreds upon hundreds of times she sat with them in the dark until they fell asleep, stroking a soft head, singing quietly, praying silently. Telling them how important and beautiful and incredible they were. Gawking over every drawing, reading through every homework assignment, bandaging every wound. *Please remember these things*, she pleads. *Remember my love, first of all and forever, that I loved you best and truest and always. And forgive me for going, I would have endured anything to stay with you.* But behind that truth there is another frightening truth. That we cannot endure everything, that eventually it is enough and our bodies, no matter how we will them to remain , eventually extinguish. We all hope and count on it being later rather than sooner, but that is not always the case.

Cancer is a life unto itself. The word is packed with meaning. Fear. That may be at the top of the list. The universal word that everyone relates to. But the journey of cancer is also the journey of life: stories, sorrow, joy, prayers. It is a strange disease. Even as I attempt to explain it to my children I recognize how strange it is. No, they will not catch it, though perhaps (and I do not tell them this) it could also lurk within them. It is something my body is doing to itself, for reasons no one fully understands. My own body has suddenly become my enemy. It is not an outside force, and so not easy to destroy. For in destroying it we must also harm ourselves. And this, I think is what makes it so hard. Our bodies must do the unnatural and tricky job of battling themselves.

In a surprising and painful way, cancer can be beautiful. It unites people, brings out the best and kindest in them. As long as they are brought to the brink and then back again it can bring life into clarity and focus. I remember at eight getting glasses and how the whole world seemed to instantly transform from a dusty haze to a sparkling green and blue brightness. Sometimes, illness can do this too.

This morning I struggled to overcome fatigue and wrestled my sheets off the bed to cart them down to the washer. I needed to rid them of the disgusting chemo that seeps from my body as I sleep and could make its poisonous way into the bodies of my children as they snuggle with me in bed. On my way back up I searched for something to read and picked up a book I read maybe ten years ago called *The Way of the Pilgrim*. In the preface I read the following words by Turgenev: "every man should write the story of his life." I have been trying for years to write many stories; stories real and make-believe, or a combination of both. But the story I know best is my own. This is a piece of it.

I am seventeen weeks pregnant and have just entered the "out of the danger zone" phase after which you are told it's okay to share the happy news with everyone. I announce it on Facebook with a picture of the kids touching my pregnant belly (a picture I still cannot bring myself to look at).

The girls and I go for a routine visit to check my vitals and weight and to hear the baby's heartbeat. I tell

Will not to bother leaving work to come, there will be plenty more visits for him to be a part of and I know it's a burden on him to get away.

But then...there is no heartbeat.

The doctor listens for a long time, then brings in the ultrasound machine. But there is nothing; the baby is gone. It looks like she died close to fifteen weeks. I hold it together, but barely, for the girls, and because I know that once I let them come the tears and horror will overwhelm me. And in the car, they do. Emma, who is only five but always understands so much, weeps too. Two weeks? How could I carry my dead baby around for two weeks and not know? And now they asked me to carry her little shriveled body for two more days, because that was when they could get me in for surgery, and when my friend Jo could watch the girls.

Sometime in mid-March we buried her. The doctor told William while I was still waking up from surgery that we had a girl. He waited until a few days later to tell me because he knew in the sometimes surprisingly sensitive way he has that it would be too much. We named her Esther Anne (after the Biblical princess and Anne Shirley). We took her tiny pink urn to a park we loved to hike in and the boys and Will dug a spot: deep in the woods, but well marked. We all helped cover it and prayed together. I don't know if this is something that will haunt the kids or if it brought closure. Quite possibly both.

Colleen, who delivered her baby girl at 33 weeks, did not live to see her turn one.

I had been seeing blood in my stool for about six

weeks and had been ignoring it despite Will's concern. By April it was bad enough for him to stuff me and all four kids in the car and march me, despite my protests, to the ER. They took a stool sample and did a CT scan but it came back clear other than a small spot on my pancreas (nothing of much concern). They sent us home but I continued to get worse.

William scheduled me for an appointment with a gastroenterologist who he knew and after discussing my symptoms she was worried enough to schedule me for a colonoscopy. Looking back, I can so easily see how things could have gone much differently for me. I am stubborn but happened to marry a man even more strong willed than me, who loved me deeply. Otherwise I surely would not have gone in until it was too late. Or, like Colleen, my symptoms would have been ignored. Later, the surgeon told us that I probably had a few weeks before the cancer would have spread to my lymphatic system and throughout my entire body.

When Will came, we wept. We were also in shock. This certainly did not seem real. But something in me took over, something powerful that wanted to live but was also okay with whatever would come of this. As I lay in the MRI machine, immobile for forty-five minutes, I willed myself not to cry but tears flowed down my cheeks nonetheless, forming pools at the sides of my face.

Will was furious that they had missed this softball-sized mass in my colon on the CT scan and marched down to radiology to have them pull up my scan. "Oh yeah," the radiologist said, "there it is."

I kept the boys home from school the day before surgery prep and Will took off from work. As always in crisis, he was gentle, kind and patient. We drove two hours to go hiking at Johnson's Shut Ins State Park and Elephant Rock Park, two places I had been longing to go to since we moved to St Louis. Since the colonoscopy I had been able to feel the mass in my colon, a constant throbbing presence. It removed my appetite and I had lost ten pounds in less than a week. Somehow though, I had the strength for this. It was a perfect day and there was hardly anyone else out on a Tuesday in April. The water was clear and cold and I felt every little breeze touch my skin, every beam of sunlight on my face. I put my fingers in Nina's soft curls and soaked in the sound of the kids' shouts and laughter. Nothing can be wrong with the world and those you love when they seem so precious. And they can not be more precious than when you understand life is precarious.

I scrubbed my hair and body with the antiseptic they had given me and went in for surgery on Thursday. I was floating: none of this was really happening to me. I think it was all so fast that there was no time to process, to mourn, to think about any of it. I did think about my children. I thought about what would happen if anything went wrong, so I wrote down some little things I wanted them to have. My wedding ring to Nina, my engagement ring to James, my grandmother's ring to Samuel, my wedding dress to Emma. Not much else that seemed worth bothering about. I wrote a little to each of them, but did not have the energy to write very much.

It was eight hours later and Easter Sunday when I woke up. I had a six inch incision across my lower abdomen and three other one inch incisions which had been used to insert the laparoscopic tools. One just above my belly button, the other two (I just checked) about six inches to the left and right of this. The one on the left had a tube coming out of it attached to a little bag which drained bright red fluid from somewhere inside me. It was not until I saw my body that I realized it would never be the same. I would have these scars forever, no smooth stomach. I looked like some sort of mutilated zombie creature. I cried over this many times during the next few weeks, silly as it seems. I felt sad that I had not even thought about how my body would be changed, not even said goodbye to or tried to remember what it felt like to be whole. But the tumor was out. This was the most important thing.

At some point in all of this my kids came to visit, along with my mother, my best friend Jo, and my priest. Because my mom was there with the kids, Will was able to stay with me the whole time. He lay in the bed next to me and occasionally reached over to take my limp hand.

Colleen's husband, unable to handle the responsibility of a sick wife, left after her diagnosis.

I felt crippled that first week home, not being able to get in and out of bed by myself. Will would gently lift me. Not able to pick up my sweet, snuggly Nina. Not being able to hug any of the children with more than the ends of my outstretched arms, not the all-encircling hugs a mother should give. Protecting my tender abdomen from the unintentional violence of their love.

I find that wherever I am, I wonder if any of the people I see have cancer. I never did this before. It can be such a strange, hidden disease, only showing itself in the most obscure ways. The line and bump of a port under the surface of the skin, an unnatural thinness or a soft roundness that comes when the thyroid is destroyed inadvertently by radiation to cancerous lymph nodes. A ghostly pallor, a wrap or hat to cover thinning or missing hair. There is a woman now sitting within my line of vision at Panera, a little to the right of me. She is so thin she almost seems translucent, and looks so old and fragile, her hair is noticeably thinning, she looks like little more than a corpse. But she is *alive*. I see her smile brightly at the child in the high chair next to her table and she talks in a quick, animated way to her friend (or daughter). I guess this disease will probably haunt me forever. I wonder how long this woman will live. Will she ever know I thought of her and said a silent prayer?

I can't figure out why but sometimes the disconnect from my pump is more difficult than anything else. First is the push of saline and blood thinner which I can feel going into my port and then I can taste the nauseating saltiness in my mouth. Next I slowly peel off all of the tape attaching the needle and tubing to my chest. Then the worst part. I grasp onto the dresser and Will pulls it out. It's usually at this point that I cry my burning chemo tears. It is so incredibly emotional having this thing removed from my body. Relief, terror, or exhaustion overwhelm me. Will does it for me, all but taking off the tape which I do. He is gentle but I am always scared that he will inadvertently hurt me.

I find that since I have no more treatments, even though it has been a meager three weeks, my mind is swiftly relegating memories to the realm of dreams. It is with effort that I recall the fatigue that made it almost impossible to get out of bed, the numbness in my hands, the terrifying cramping in my neck and face, the cold-induced shock in my mouth and throat. I try to remember them though, because it seems necessary. It is strange that already I can only remember what was meaningful. I think, in a way my life has not seemed worth fighting for in a long time. It brought clarity to the intervening days, brought life into focus, relationships too. The children were kind, I felt loved, attended to. The weakness of my body seemed to me a mountain to climb every time, a necessary challenge. Yes, of course I dreaded it, spent days before in a state of anxiety, but those feelings seem to be leaving me while the memory of being important for a while has not. I felt my existence necessary, my presence a boon to my family, my absence a suffering. Already they have forgotten too, take everything for granted again, as I suppose families do. I do not want my children to fear for me, do not want them to see me sick with fatigue, but it also brought out the best in them and in me.

I want the fact that I have survived this to mean something. What does it mean?

It would mean something to Colleen.

It is pouring right now, and the children are screaming happily, drenched, bouncing on the trampoline. I love them so much my heart could burst. My gut bubbles with joy listening to them. They do complete me, and often it is enough.

Sometimes I imagine them as they will be many years from now, maybe long after my body rots in the earth. What will their faces become? I often study old men and women trying to see a glimpse of my children, after they have lived fully, or even to see myself in them. The drooping and graying of flesh under the eyes, under the chin, the sides of the cheeks pocketing and sagging. The eyes still bright, but hidden in innumerable creases. The face is mainly what I see. It is the first sign of age, the rest of the body can stay hidden in fabric, the hands too, spotted, calloused, bony and strewn with veins. I want to cry when I picture Nina as this apparition. Her soft, round, rosy, joyful body crumpled, her affectionate cooing replaced with the rasp of age. But I want to know this woman, the one she will become, the one who has lived a full life, full of small and large heartaches and joys, full of memories. I want to know everything about her, and hold her and stroke her hair just as I do now, kissing the soft creases of her aged face. I also want to know myself, to banish fear of this transformation, to welcome it even, if that is possible. I see myself alone in the pew at church. William is long gone from my side but still a constant presence because the memories, smells, tastes, sounds of him will never leave. And I will see continuously the ghosts of my children, young beside me, needing me, my nourishment, my touch, my discipline and conversation and closeness. Longing and longing to be with them as we are now.

For Colleen

And her daughter, Adeline, who is one today

10. THE RAPTURE OF THE DEEP

Nicholas Finn took a pencil from the junk drawer by the kitchen table and began to sketch. Two long lines for the geothermal hot spring, one thin arched line for the dome of heat rising out of it, and a quick series of squiggles for the writhing bodies of the tube worms protruding from its surface, like the wild windswept head of Medusa. As an afterthought, he turned the pencil on its side and shaded in the area around the worms, as if each had a dark halo. "There," he said, pleased, surveying his work, "No Picasso, but I think it gives you the idea." Beth studied the picture, a wrinkle of concentration appearing on her smooth, broad forehead, below a line of straight, brown bang.

"Is that the bacteria?" she asked, pointing at the dark halo.

"Yes, it's what we think protects the worms from such high temperatures. The heat can reach as much as 700 degrees. And is full of noxious gasses."

"What's *noxious*?" Beth asked.

"Poisonous," replied Nicholas, tousling her hair. "How about I make us some popcorn? Then I can try to find the National Geographic that has the photograph I told you about. I know it's in the pile somewhere."

But Beth knew it wasn't. She knew because the mother had made her throw them out just yesterday. The pile was so tall it teetered to one side and when the baby was playing in the living room he had knocked it over on himself. Mother found him crying like a wounded bird and rather than picking him up and soothing him in her arms, had become livid about the magazines. She began tossing them frantically in all directions, ripping pages in a fretful rage. All those beautiful pages. Pictures of whales descending in a stream of blue, translucent bubbles rising from their backs, orangutans huddled under huge gnarled trees in a green swamp, an endless field of sunflowers with a pink mountain rising in the distance, a single hummingbird perched on a slim, curved stick hanging over a white waterfall. They fluttered down around the baby who had stopped crying to watch. The girl ran in when she heard the screaming and crying, tried to catch the pages before they fell, as if she knew that, when they touched the ground, they would be lost to her. Then the mother turned her anger to the girl. "Pick these up!" she screeched, "I want them out, all of them! It's absurd. He doesn't even look at them! And look what his hoarding did to the baby." The girl glanced at the baby, who seemed perfectly happy, sucking on the corner of a torn page she had not managed to save.

"No," she said. And knew it to be a mistake the moment she said it. The mother slapped her across the face, leaving a large red welt, an imprint of palm and five fingers, that would not fade for several days. The hot tears squeezed from her eyes and she dutifully gathered up all the magazines and torn pages into the white drawstring garbage bag the mother gave her. She was still crying as she dragged it out to the dumpster in the alley behind the house. Still crying as she hoisted it over her head and into the bin. She had not tied the bag and two magazines fell out, the corner of one hitting her sharply in the head. Full of rebellion, she tucked these under her shirt and dashed with them to her bedroom. She spent most of the rest of the day looking at them, and so this is how she knew, the photograph her father looked for, was gone.

This was the first betrayal of her father. The second would not happen for another twelve years.

The same year as the magazine incident, her birthday fell on a Saturday so the mother planned a little party. Emma-Lee and Brenda, who were in her class at school, and whose mothers were on the school board, were invited over for cake and ice cream. They were not really her friends, but they were nice enough, and Beth was excited about the prospect of dessert, which she was rarely allowed to have. It was a beautiful vanilla cake, frosted with a light pink buttercream and dusted in silver glitter. There were ten slim white candles in a small circle on top and the words *Happy birthday to our little cherub*. She thought that was a tad silly, but the cake was perfect otherwise. Mother cut two large slices for the other children, and one that was half that size for the girl. Her father saw the unfairness on her face and protested "It's her birthday. She can have a bigger piece, can't she?"

"It's a slippery slope," the mother hissed in a voice meant for him, but that the girl could still hear," we have to help her have self-control."

The mother had told the children not to bring gifts and had also told the girl that the party was her present from her parents, and so she was surprised and pleased when her father pulled a small gold box from his pocket. "What is this?" said mother, looking accusingly at him, "I thought we agreed, the party was enough. There's no need to spoil the child."

"It's OK," he replied, winking mischievously at Beth, "it's something useful. Go ahead, try to guess."

The box was the size of her palm and felt heavier than she would have expected something so small to feel. She held it, turning it this way and that, feeling its weight. "Is it a necklace?"

"No," he said, grinning now, "think outside the box." She considered longer this time before answering.

"A key?"

"No," but that's a better guess. "Girls, why don't you help her? What do you think?"

"A little toy horse?" Brenda said, shyly.

"A charm bracelet?" said Emma-Lee.

"A wooden car!"

"Coins!"

"Marbles!"

"Earrings!"

"A locket!"

The girls shouted over each other in their excitement. Her father was laughing now, a joyful, rolling, carefree, boyish sound.

"No, no," he said, between his laughter. "Shall we have her open it now?"

"Yes!" all three children squealed at once. Beth looked at her father.

"Go ahead," he said, nodding at her.

Carefully, she peeled back the tape from the side of the box and lifted the lid. Inside, nestled in a foamy pillow, was a watch. The face was royal blue bordered by pale sapphire. The minute and hour hands were silver and the second-hand scarlet. On the watch face was stamped the word 'Seiko'.

"Oh my God Nicky," the mother gasped, "what have you done?"

It was a $900 dive watch.

Beth could not remember a time when she had not

wanted to dive. It seemed to be something that came to her in the womb. A place, she imagined, not unlike the deep. A familiar world, silent but for the rush of blood echoing through the ear canal, the cool slick of water on skin, the freedom of weightlessness. Even the first time, she was not afraid. It was also, of course, her father's world.

Nicholas came to marine biology as a matter of course. His love affair with the sea began as a child growing up on Little Cayman, a dime-sized island in the Caribbean used almost exclusively for diving. His mother owned a small dive shop where she lived and worked. "My mother and father were the sea, my teacher, my priest, my friends. I didn't need anything else. At least that's what I thought," he would tell her, with a sideways smile. "Then you came, and changed everything." She would grin at that and snuggle in close to him. He even smelled like the sea: briny and sweet.

In 1973 he completed a master's degree in geology and courses to certify him as a level 3 technical and cave diver. He had spent his life since then exploring the world's oceans. Handsome and jovial, he made friends easily and his knowledge, combined with a certain joie de vivre, earned him some small fame. Sometimes his work took him away for months and Beth lived each day waiting for his return and for the story that would accompany it.

When Beth was five he went to Tiger Beach, Grand Bahama to swim with and study sharks. "At first," he said as she rested her head on his shoulder, "I was nervous, there were hundreds of sharks and I could see them circling in the water. The water there is so clear you can almost see straight to the bottom. Some of them were sharks known for being particularly aggressive. I could see lemon, tiger, and hammerhead sharks all from the deck of the boat."

"What did you do, Daddy?"

"Of course, I couldn't back down. Everyone was watching me. So, I took a deep breath and pictured you. I pictured telling you about it just like this. And then I jumped."

"Oh, Daddy."

"And you know what? As soon as I was in the water all my fear went away. They were such beautiful creatures and they just swam around, checking me out. The guys who go out there all the time told me it's best to get down quickly so you're out of their feeding zone. So that's what I did. And I was also careful not to let them get their noses right under me. They have an instinct to open their jaws and bite if their nose is at a particular angle to you—Like this!" When he said that, he ducked under her arm and picked her up, spinning her around in a circle, tickling her until she laughed so much her tummy ached.

When she was eight he had his big break, discovering a nudibranch, or sea slug, that looked just like a small white bunny. The photographs of it quickly spread around the globe and suddenly he was inundated with calls to join various expeditions. He travelled even more, but she never minded, because when he returned, he always had another story: Following giant sea turtles off the coast of Egypt, swimming in a 60,000-year-old prehistoric sea forest of Bald Cypress, descending into the Great Blue Hole in Belize. Each adventure seemed more marvelous than the last.

Once, he came home and told her the story of a

diver who acquired a brain-eating amoeba in a fresh-water spring, realized it was going to kill him and strapped on a tank and a pile of weights and descended over The Wall, a 10,000-foot drop-off in the Caribbean. This story frightened and fascinated her. It seemed to hold the same bizarre fascination for her father.

The mother never learned to dive. She was afflicted by claustrophobia, and even terrified to have her head beneath a blanket. She forbade Nicholas from taking the girl, saying she was afraid something would happen to her only daughter. The girl knew it was not out of fear of her safety, but out of jealousy that she forbade it. Nicholas said simply and quietly:“ we'll see, we'll see.” And for some reason Beth never learned, when the time came, when she was old enough, the mother let them dive and never spoke of her misgivings again.

When Beth was twenty-two, her father invited her to go on a dive trip with him to Eagles Nest, a fresh-water cavern in Florida. Her father was one of the last people to dive there before the death of a local father and son, and the ensuing public outcry, caused it to be closed for ten years. The theory was that they had succumbed to nitrogen narcosis, more poetically known as “the rapture of the deep,” where nitrogen builds up in the blood to a level that effectively intoxicates the divers, giving them a sense of euphoria and immortality that causes them to recklessly descend ever deeper. Now, the cavern was finally opening up again and he wanted to be one of the first to return. The cave entrance was almost three hundred feet below the surface and extended in over a mile of hive-like caverns. As far as anyone knew there was only one way in or out. In order to dive to this depth and stay for any period of time they would need to be on closed circuit rebreathers, which would allow them to recycle unused oxygen, staying down for as much as twenty hours. For this first dive, they planned to stay for only four. Four hours at such a depth, however, would require ten hours of decompression, in order to resurface safely without risk of air bubbles forming in their blood stream.

Beth now had two children of her own. Her husband was busy with work, so her father bought their tickets to Florida from New Jersey, and mother reluctantly agreed to come and watch the children. That morning she said a quick goodbye to mother, gave the accompanying hugs and kisses to the children, and eagerly jumped into the front of her dad's white pick-up. It was not until they were down the gravel drive and nearly to the main road that she thought to turn around and give one last wave. By then, she could barely see them.

It was a two-hour drive from the house to Eagles Nest and Beth sat with the window down, her eyes half closed, basking in the sun, the sounds of Marley and Dylan, and her father's voice. "Wait till you see it, it's so unassuming, just another little Florida lake, and then there's this whole world under there, miles of it. Can you imagine, the first person that discovered that? How amazing that must have been." She listened and smiled. The excitement in his voice was contagious.

It was almost ten when they arrived at the white dirt road winding towards the lake. It was obvious no one had been out recently since they had to stop twice to move debris from their path. The lake was unassuming, not much more than a gray-blue pond circled by bright green Bald Cypress, like a ring of overgrown Christmas

Trees. They parked and stood in silence for a moment, paying their respects, drinking in the above-ground image, as they always did before a dive. The water, he had taught her, was always to be respected, the land and the air never to be taken for granted. Then they proceeded to put on their equipment. Over the years they had accumulated top of the line gear and her father had meticulously checked everything before they left the house. Masks and backup masks, lights and backup lights, BC's, regulators, tanks, aqua pencil and slate, fins, wetsuits, line, and of course her Seiko dive watch, which she hardly ever removed. When they were ready, they waded together into the warm lake water and swam out to the center. Then they began their descent.

The water was clear and warm but she could feel the temperature drop quickly as her gloveless hands ached with cold. They never wore gloves cave diving since it was important to have access to the sense of touch, the only truly reliable thing in such an environment. When she first trained in cave-diving, the test where her mask was blinded and she had to navigate with only the line was the most difficult. She almost failed it. Now, after dozens of cave-dives, relying on touch (the smooth feel of the line in her palm, the cold water sliding over her skin) was second nature. It took them five minutes to descend the three hundred feet to the cave entrance. At the entrance was a sign with a picture of the grim reaper and the words: *Prevent your death. Go no further*. Her father looked at her and raised his eyebrows. She knew they were thinking the same thing. Anyone who came this far was never going to be deterred by that.

Inside, the cave opened up into a massive chamber

known as The Ballroom, which was where they would spend ten hours decompressing on their way back up, but for now they swam quickly through it, and into one of the small tunnel offshoots, their line unraveling behind them.

Her father let her lead the way, choosing where they would go, and she simply went wherever she had the desire. Occasionally she checked her watch to see their depth, and how much oxygen they had used, but mostly she meandered through the tunnels, turning this way and that, with no thought of time or space, sometimes looking back to meet her father's smiling eyes.

The light from their headlamps made the cavern glow neon-green and amber. There was almost no current and if they were careful not to disturb the silty bottom with their fins, the visibility was almost endless, reaching as far as the light did.

Sometimes, he tugged on her fin and pointed. Once, to a formation of rock, clusters of round, tubular shapes that reminded her of the worms from his stories; another time, to a double-sided dome that looked like two parted lips. Sometimes she turned to point something out to him that was ahead or to the side and he had not seen yet.

Almost two hours in, she came to a sort of crossroads. Ahead was a solid wall of rock; to the right was a shaft that dropped down into unknown depths, and to the left was an even smaller opening, smooth-walled and also seeming to plummet out of sight. The entrance on the right was narrow, but not as much as the one on the left; she thought she could squeeze through by turning slightly on her side, and angling her tank between her legs. Her father was too far back for her to ask his opinion and she was anxious to cover as much ground as she could in the time they had. Slowly, she began wriggling her body back and forth, squeezing first her head, then her shoulders and back through the opening. It was not until it reached her hips, where the tank was wedged, that she had any difficulty. Now, she found, no matter which way she turned, she could not seem to get the rest of her body through. Neither could she go back the way she had come. The bulk of the tank was inflexible, and although her body could curve and bend between the rock, the tank could not. After a few minutes she felt her father come up behind her and, grabbing hold of her legs, try to pull her backward towards him, and when that did not work, push her forward, through the tunnel. But as the tank was immovable, so was the rock. She did not budge, only cried out silently as the rock ground into her flesh, and the grip of her fathers 'fingers dug into her legs.

They continued to try and get her out for almost an hour, and she was calm until they approached the three-hour mark. This was the time they had planned to turn back, and the oxygen they had was with this in mind. Her mind was reeling. She could not think of what to do. She could feel the short, sharp intakes of breath that meant she was hyperventilating, using up even more precious oxygen.

Then suddenly, she was free, being pulled back and held by strong arms. For a moment she couldn't breathe, and felt feather-light, instinct and training kicked in, keeping her from panic. The cave was full of silt they had stirred in their attempt to pry her loose, and she could see nothing, but she could still feel. She could feel a tank being strapped to her back, and a regulator shoved in her mouth, and then she was heavy and she could breathe once more. She could see her father now; his mask was inches from hers, but he had no tank and was breathing with the extra regulator on her BC. He took out a pencil and slate from a pocket and began to write.

He was calm. Medical. He wrote slowly, carefully, so she could read it, and there would be no mistaking what he had written.

GO

I cut your tank free

No O2 for both of us

I love you

She read it twice, three times, five times—but she could not understand what it said. Finally, he took her face in his hands and lifted it, so she was looking at him. His eyes were shining, but not with tears. She shook her head violently at him, then she erased what he ad written and wrote.

NO.

Can buddy breathe

But here her thoughts trailed off. It was impossible. There was no way for them to decompress on the oxygen from one tank. She erased what she had written and wrote simply:

WONT LEAVE U

He looked at her for a long moment, then, before she could understand what he was doing, he removed the regulator from his mouth, dropped the line, and slid through the same tunnel on the right, emptying the air from his BC and turning off his light in one swift motion. Instantly, he disappeared from sight. She screamed, but it made no sound. She pushed herself to the mouth of the tunnel and reached through with her light, but there was nothing to see but black water dropping away endlessly, until it vanished with the last of the light. She could not even see the faintest shape of him.

She had no choice but to go back.

And so she did.

A team of four professional divers searched for a month for his body. It was never found. Neither was the tank she had lost. The state issued a death certificate anyway, and the funeral was held the following week.

There were too many people. She wanted it to just be her and him. Everyone else seemed like an intruder. And yet, she knew they were honoring him, honoring his life, honoring what he had done for her. For that, she was grateful.

She thought her mother would blame her, for she was to blame. But her mother only said in a calm, far-away voice, "he made his own choices." Then, she hugged her daughter, and they both cried.

Later, she came to understand her mother, in a way she never tried to before. Her loneliness, in doing the job of raising two children on her own. A husband who they looked to as a god, and her who they saw as judge and jury on their lives. Beth understood her mother did the best she could. She also saw her father as something both more and less than he had been. A man who loved his family, but often chose the sea first. Who, in a way, even in his death, had chosen that last great frontier. The unknown blue. The rapture of the deep.

ACKNOWLEDGEMENT

All my thanks to my parents, Lynn and Tony, who first gave me the gift of love for the written word; to my friends Joanna and Bryant, who make me feel less alone in the world; to my brothers, Aaron and Joel, who were my childhood co-conspirators, our adventures the impetus to a wild imagination and a trove of stories; to my editor, Alejandro, whose attention to detail was just what was needed; to my talented daughter, Helen, who did the beautiful interior artwork; and to my sweet puppy, Alice, who tirelessly kept me company. And to you, dear reader, without whom this would not exist.

ABOUT THE AUTHOR

Rebecca Matthew

Rebecca is a mother adventurer, and storyteller who can never get enough of the sea and night sky. Her work appears in several literary journals, magazines, and collections, and her debut novel is forthcoming. She is thrilled you've joined her on one of the greatest adventures of all—reading.

Made in the USA
Columbia, SC
01 August 2025

1f3ddd78-eb05-48f7-b686-bdb94bb6c99eR01